Naked Among the Tombs

NAKED AMONG THE TOMBS

A novel

Nicholas Philliou

iUniverse, Inc.
New York Lincoln Shanghai

Naked Among the Tombs
A novel

Copyright © 2005 by Nicholas Philliou

All rights reserved. No part of this book may be used or reproduced by any means, graphic, electronic, or mechanical, including photocopying, recording, taping or by any information storage retrieval system without the written permission of the publisher except in the case of brief quotations embodied in critical articles and reviews.

iUniverse books may be ordered through booksellers or by contacting:

iUniverse
2021 Pine Lake Road, Suite 100
Lincoln, NE 68512
www.iuniverse.com
1-800-Authors (1-800-288-4677)

ISBN-13: 978-0-595-36146-5 (pbk)
ISBN-13: 978-0-595-80590-7 (ebk)
ISBN-10: 0-595-36146-3 (pbk)
ISBN-10: 0-595-80590-6 (ebk)

Printed in the United States of America

Study the Way and never grow old
distrust emotions, truth will emerge
sweep away your worries
set even your body aside
Autumn drives off the yellow leaves
yet Spring renews each green bud
quietly contemplate the pattern of things
nothing here to make us sad.

—Shih-Shu

CONTENTS

▼

Introduction: Poetry..ix

Chapter 1: Full of Water 1

Chapter 2: Waking Up Scared 5

Chapter 3: Sunday Night Blues 14

Chapter 4: Through the Looking Hat 20

Chapter 5: Things Greater Than Tai Chi 28

Chapter 6: Back to the Grind 39

Chapter 7: Hall of Illusion 51

Chapter 8: Detachment.. 63

Chapter 9: Take Only Pictures 81

Chapter 10: Runner, Digger, Listener 88

Chapter 11: Claw Marks in the Sky 101

Chapter 12: The Narrow Road to the Deep North 115

Chapter 13: Joy to the Word.. 153

Introduction: Poetry

This small leather-bound book fits neatly into my pocket. When seen writing in it, the sleek-looking pad helps me fit into the style of a professional citizen with a busy schedule. I would imagine that it makes me appear organized, an individual who checks off daily successes. Its slight weight is comforting and its true purpose private.

Blank pages are always within my grasp. My secret canvas is unconditional, a wonderful emptiness to spew out insecurities, memories, or any mumbled imaginings from my inner mind. The management agencies that know everything about me—from my eye color to my current location—are not privy to my journal. Sometimes, I feel like a poet trapped in a common person's life.

It seems strange that a dusty, wrinkled postcard, now tacked to my bedroom wall, could arouse the need to open this book and to put together paper and pen over and over again. A faded photograph of an American desert with the note, "*When you're ready, you're always welcome*" was the simple catalyst for all this inner dialogue.

*   *   *   *

I grew up with anxiety. As a kid I believed that some final battle between good and evil was going to take place in my lifetime. Armageddon was imminent because my brother Basil told me so. Older siblings are role models who are often burdened with the important responsibility of passing on sacred knowledge, and mine took his job very seriously.

We made obstacle courses in the woods so that we could train to evade New World Order invaders and asked Santa to give us army surplus gear for Christmas. We strained and sweated while doing commando exercises pulled from the pages of *Soldier of Fortune* magazines. In fact, Basil convinced our Boy Scout troop to go paramilitary, and weekend overnights often turned into covert training ops. Plants harvested from sidewalk cracks slid easily between peanut butter and jelly sandwiches and helped us get used to the sustenance of survival living. We dissected heavy-metal lyrics in search of important hidden apocalyptic messages. When the ozone layer was confirmed holey we painted ourselves in clay, became amateur cavers, and tried to adapt to nocturnal living by staying up all night and consuming carrots by the bushel to improve our night vision. We really did this stuff, and there were no limits to how far our fantasy could take us.

Every major storm was the beginning of the end: any minor catastrophe was the Horsemen of the Apocalypse arriving. All the prophecies and conspiracies swirled in my brother's blender and were poured out for me as a paranoid concoction that no ten-year-old should sip from. I was prayerful, quiet, and very serious. I loved it though, because I was a kid, and the gift of children is that just about anything can be made it into a game. I was committed to winning by being a future survivor of mankind's defining era.

In 1999, I was thirteen, and for the first time I could see that there were more than a handful of people believing that the lights were about to go out for good. Folks were stockpiling, and our familiar fear that kept us sharp and well-trained was becoming a national hysteria. I will not forget Basil's happiness as Mom stuffed the cabinets with oats and bottled water. She said it was "just in case," but when we unloaded canned goods from the trunk of her car our game suddenly had adult meaning.

Humanity's pride and arrogance and false faith in technology would be our undoing. Computer programmers were the unconscious architects of the end of the world. When the calendar changed to 2000 and the computer systems that ran the world read it as 1900, all hell was going to break loose. Prison doors were going to fling open, and refrigeration would break down. As helicopters lifelessly dropped from the sky and the New Year's ball sat impotent in Time's Square, the humble visionaries that we were would be ready.

Our backpacks were packed. We would take care of the family as long as we could. If the suburbs were overrun by starving and dehydrated lawless mobs, we had consigned ourselves in a secret pact and a harsh shot of Dad's ouzo to go on; someone had to rebuild the broken world when the smoke cleared. When shit truly hit the fan, and cops began blowing people away for their last baked bean and wild dogs crazed from biting through laboratory cages came for revenge, we were going to beeline it on foot to the safe zones, deep into wilderness.

Our youngest brother was seven and would come with us. He was small and wouldn't require much food. Our parents would have to make up their own minds and if by some miracle they chose to follow us, would have to hold their own on open trails as we moved like shadows protecting them and other old people who came to sanity at the eleventh hour. Like Robin Hoods we could hunt deer and rabbit to feed their aching bellies and wouldn't be emotionally swayed by their tears of joy and apologies for not listening all along.

Alexander, the firstborn in the Cast family, was still in denial and had the gall to plan on hosting a Y2K party where he could charge ten bucks a head—five if you were a girl. The fool, we thought. We had done it. It was all coming together, and Alex's party ideas typified the thinking that made this terrible, wonderful moment possible.

✳   ✳   ✳   ✳

The anti-climax of the new millennium was the straw that broke my paranoia, and one of the last times I saw Basil. Even when he was right in front of me, he wasn't really there. He kept searching for the future in chaos and grew uncomfortable with stability. The System wasn't breaking fast enough and he hated its endurance.

I suppose that Basil decided to become the post-apocalyptic survivor he had prepared to be. Anarchy was his passion. He aided radical causes right and left, freed animals, smashed corporate coffee shop windows, monkey-wrenched productivity, stood in front of chainsaws to save trees and gritted his teeth in the face of mace and bulletproof shields for the rights of small farmers. He shunned any entertainment resembling the new and progressive and chose instead to listen to old jam bands and grit-toothed folk music. When not manic with revolution, he became withdrawn. He sat for hours in our suburban backyard, tormented by the whine of landscaping machines and refusing to enter a house where televisions pumped out propaganda.

He finished high school with a bang, leaving the graduation ceremony in handcuffs after blowing up the podium with a shoebox full of M-80s. Hanging his head, he was not proud of what he had done but still made it seem necessary to do. Angry kids cheered him but he just shook his head in silence. I could almost hear his thoughts speaking to everyone: *you all don't get it.* Everyone but me, of course.

The backpack, once reserved for emergency, became his new home. It seemed his search would never end. By the time our country was attacked by terrorists

Basil was gone—off the grid, I presumed, and hopefully out of trouble. I stopped thinking about Armageddon so much and went on my own trip. My mind became quiet and I let the world in. Seriousness was never again to exceed relaxation, and I found ways to balance the scales. I graduated from college with a degree in philosophy. I got this job I take a train to, and have a girlfriend to hang out with and a best friend I share a place with.

Basil's been out West for a while, and the postcard seemed, although brief, to exude that old prophetic confidence which ignites in me a dormant alert feeling. "When you're ready," he writes, "you're always welcome." When I'm ready, I'll be welcome? What does that mean? Is there a hidden message about the shit going down? Or am I just reading something into a simple invitation?

Everyone is anxious to some degree about the future, and for many nuclear, biological, natural and psychotic good reasons. Although I might not have a survival kit under my bed, I do still sit up and think occasionally. Sometimes I turn the light on just before the sun comes up so that I can write something down. I love poetry because, like Basil, it need not conform to the common rules. The poems are my priest, shaman, and therapist; they are my way of dealing with consciousness and interpreting messages that come from far away.

CHAPTER 1

▼

FULL OF WATER

*These are the types of poems
that can get a man killed,
so if something does happen to me
don't bother launching an investigation,
read the poems
and find out
why they needed to do it.*

*　　　*　　　*　　　*

The subway station was an aquifer for underground human energy, and I entered it with all the others. Like detritus floating toward a fish's mouth, my body moved without excitement. Somehow among the great morning commotion, with hundreds of people bumping and bowing and making their way to or from the bread basket, everything was silent. My awareness was as low as the rats beneath the rails, and I wasn't ready for anything more than a dronelike walk to work. The open air was upstairs, and I looked forward to a breeze that might wake me. What happened next turned out to be more of a wake-up then I ever wanted.

An unexpected sound fired through space. A gruff group of letters that made up a word crackled the air like something shot from a pistol. It made its mark on the back of my head and sent shock waves through my feet.

"Cone-stan-teen!"

It made me lose my balance, yanking me as violently as an undertow. He was using my real name. I am Constantine Cast; it's on my birth certificate. My friends call me Gus, my mom calls me Costa, but nobody calls me Constantine. Woozily, I turned around.

When I faced him I realized the screamer was an Asian kid whom I recognized from my train ride. During this morning's commute he had been quietly moving to a beat delivered from large 70s-style headphones. A college student, I supposed, perhaps younger. Retro clothes, dyed hair, one of those brooding Japanese James Dean types. Now he was screaming for me, at me, in public, on the station floor. Loud too, louder than any voice I ever heard before. People in the vicinity instinctively covered their ears. He must have been using some sort of practiced scream to get my attention because I was physically affected. (I would learn later that it was the Water Word Technique of the *Mizu-ryu*, a part of his assassin's arsenal.)

Not sure how to greet the stranger, and for some reason unable to speak, I raised my hand in a universal gesture of "what's up?" This must have been a cultural faux pas, because his body looked charged with anger. To my utter shock his headphones hit the ground and his foot shot through the air. The sneaker he wore might as well have been covering an iron bar, because as it hit just below my sternum air rushed from my face like a bellows and my body toppled as if I were a bag of wet leaves.

Careening backward and clutching my midsection, I took in a scene of controlled panic. Everybody was leaving, as they should—as we are taught to do in Emergency Management commercials. Get out of the potentially dangerous scene and get help.

Silence again. Just me and Tada. (Yoshitsuru Tada according to the police report. A gang member aspiring to move up in the ranks of organized crime by completing a contract on UFSA soil.) He settled into the platform and stared intently at my collapsed skeleton, assessing and preparing his next move. I tried to pull in air, like sucking through a stirring straw.

This guy had me on my knees with one lightning-fast kick. What could I do? Go fetal and let him introduce his foot to my face? Stand up? To run I had to rise. He watched me come to one knee and for some reason gave me that moment to stand. At last, after fully up, adrenaline shot through my veins in realization. He wanted a bigger target.

He charged and left the ground in one birdlike leap. His legs felt like metal cables as they locked viselike around my torso. He slammed his forehead into my nose while simultaneously thumping the areas below my ears with the meaty knife-edges of his hands.

The sound of an ocean wave breaking and the feeling of water cascading through every limb made me stop struggling. My bladder and bowels released their contents in one moment of total surrender. My body collapsed for a second time and Tada stood again, grounding himself and observing predatorily. His thin black eyes showed emotion for the first time, shock that I was not completely extinguished. He inched forward and began to strangle me with my own collar. The life was leaving me. It all happened so fast. But this is the new New York, and police response times are two minutes maximum in a subway terminal.

Blurry vision and the sound of the sea made my coming death almost peaceful. A form that cast a shadow upon my attacker seemed angelic, and for me, signaled the end. Perhaps the Grim Reaper was for real, and his scythe was about to swoop down. Before I could whisper parting prayers the ethereal suddenly became very real, than catlike!

The shadow belonged to a strange old man I talked with this morning. This really proper guy was swinging his cane toward Tada's legs. The stick sliced the air and toppled the killer. The strike pulled the carpet out from under the strangler. He slammed backward but instinctively tucked his chin into his chest to avoid concussion. Tada sprang up and drove the shock from his body with a loud "*kiai!*" aimed at the old man.

The gentleman in the raggedy tan suit smiled, his thin leathery lips revealed teeth, his fangs protruded and exposed a primal powerful nature that the assassin's screams could not unbalance. My assailant seemed both confused by this vigilante and aware of his failure each time I breathed. Someone was going to die on this platform.

In that moment I remembered clearly a passage from a book called *Hidden Leaves*:

> The Way of the Samurai is in desperateness. Ten men or more cannot kill such a man. Common sense will not accomplish great things. Simply become insane and desperate.

Warrior-code bullshit, I guessed, but probably something someone like Tada grew up on. Fanaticism helped people like this survive painful initiations and have indestructible loyalty. He wasn't robbing me; someone's dirty work was being done, and karate-killers like this didn't come cheap. A professional empty-hand hit on me, an average guy, didn't make sense, but neither did octogenarians who could fight like Bruce Lee.

The old man gently crossed his arms over his chest. With outstretched fingers and the raised cane, he purposefully exposed his own midsection. He was inviting the deadly toe-kick that had made me go down. I was witnessing a wizard with unimaginable courage, yet wrapped in the tattered rags of modernity. His worn-out bowler hat and torn up shoes disguised a man foreign to the world I lived in. This was someone who channeled true power, who stood before an attacker like Moses before the lightning-filled sky.

Time must have been ticking away in the hit man's mind. He thrust a desperate and powerful kick that shattered the tile of the subway wall behind where the man-magician once stood. The screeching of an incoming train filled our ears. Two minutes had passed since the citizens evacuated the crime area.

Tada looked at me and appeared repulsed, not at the blood and excrement that covered me, but at the very life that I still struggled to hold onto inside of my heaving chest. He turned his head in confusion at the disappearance of my defender while the screech got closer and amplified.

Where was the old man, I wondered? Back in the Justice League shelter with other homeless superheroes? The kid's eyes were fearful now. Did he believe that the heat of battle could give a man sight beyond average sight? Perhaps he wondered if he had seen a demon.

Then they came, one from each side. Two SAMURAI moved at nearly inhuman speeds, running, pumping limbs with single focus and intent to incapacitate this villain. The train was just a hair closer than these cops.

Loyal to his vows and committed to his actions the young gangster leaped one last time, high and fast into the oncoming train.

*   *   *   *

One officer squatted near me in attendance of my injuries while the other tracked the crime like a well-trained bloodhound in a scene full of blood. They were the elite Secular Army Marshals Under Right and Authority International. Gently passing a palm an inch above my injured skull the New World cop removed his black sunglasses and spoke softly to his comrade in the international tongue, *"Plena de akvo."* His partner acknowledged his quick study. *"Jes, plena de akvo."*

CHAPTER 2

▼

WAKING UP SCARED

Repeating your name
trying to find its most comfortable pronunciation
a mantra has formed
with it—I am joined by unexpected images
of you.
I have
nothing
matters
of importance
no longer concern me
truly
wars rage
and I pray for the suffering
yet Gaia theory
makes sense to me
and balance need not be explained
evil is giving orders
and Babylon will grow
but your name...
when I say it
lets me sit in peace
inside a cube
cool shadows cover me

and the people who legally rob my energies must
rest from their hungers.
Sleepy, dreamy
oh Canada
your crisp snow covered trees seem imaginary
where will I be?
half blind, voracious from hibernation?
and all I have to do
seems to have nothing to do with thee-
worldly world
and it is hard
to keep to the attainment of unrespectable goals
tears can flavor
comfort soup and burn whip marks
so tired of pretending
the Christians
where are they?
smelling of honey
eating locusts
receiving the vision
is a trip
making one unfit for work, for school, for
bullshit
orange jump suits
and gangs
balance the scales
of the slave machine
and peace and practicality
oppose each other
and I can't stop blaming someone else.
I am finding myself
in liquid thoughts
and thinning hair.
Poets are sad sacks
who cry too easily
and laugh too little.
What is so damned important?
about people's eyes?

moist with longing
anyone and everyone you will ever meet
has the eyes of a child
harboring in them some concept known as Soul
hazel, blue, green, brown, yellow and black
with speckles
the pupil fascinates me
growing large when tripping
'look at my eyes
am I still tripping?'
with dumb questions
comes horrifying dialogue
leading to lies and sports talk
and salary-men screwing hot coaled barbecues
with beer soaked phalluses
I want to take the trip
a sharp
large pupil
tearing away from all things phony
and freaking out at childhood house things
that's why I need to leave it all behind.
the desert of somewhere out there
awaits my tripping stare and bare feet
my right foot is stuffed with sand and
ball bearings but the toilet seat is better
than out there where
I cannot sit, or think
without being disturbed by the imbalance
of TV faces, stupid clothes, consumer deities,
the devil's minions, married rapists, child madness,
old age madness, dyed hair, hair plugs, hair weaves, hair growth drugs, snake oil,
tortuous thoughts, working jobs no one likes, crying to office workers in code
with that same sad, trying,
unknowingly, unconsciously,
immorally prying, and without honesty,
unreflective, self-deprecating,
evil eyed contemptuously wishing
bad jealous evil things

dreading the loneliness of times to come
pressing in on the power button with your pointing finger
the bit byte chirping is transferred
straight through you into cold movable flabby storage
'got any big plans for the weekend?'
a mantra has formed
when I say it
cool shadows cover me.

Waking up wet from the storms of nightmares, I was alert enough to know I was in a hospital room. Pain stabbed below my ears, and searching the room with my eyes was traumatic. As if I were shrunken and put inside a fishbowl, everything I looked at was distorted. A house of mirrors within each eye. A face enlarged and overwhelming charged my gaze and I heard myself scream, "*aaaah-hhh!*" A disturbing caricature of someone I knew. Like missing the last step on a staircase in the dark, my heart skipped and I prayed for a light switch.

"Gus, calm down, it's me Wyeth!"

Neederman. At last, some sanity. I'm still not opening my eyes. My comprehending mind was comforted by my best friend's presence, but I've done enough drugs to know how to respect freaky hallucinations. My orbits were staying shut until I found out what the fuck was going on.

"Wyeth...." I spoke with a saliva coated lower lip. "You looked all fucked up."

He was hesitating, oh shit, did I offend him? He couldn't really look like the Pumpkin-head. How bad did I look? Neederman was deep breathing to get a grip. He got closer, I could feel his body heat. Laid his arm across my chest gently, trying to be comforting I suppose. His breath was near my ear, he was going to whisper, something must be up if he wanted to keep it secret.

"No Gus...it's you who's fucked up."

"What!" I grasped the sheet beneath me in panic.

"Calm down, you're gonna be ok, but...you took some serious wallops to your noggin, and...and...."

I was taking it all in pretty coolly, all things considered, but Neederman had to finish his thought or I was going to open my eyes again.

"What is it Wye, what else?"

He bent closer, and he must've had a Mexican omelet for breakfast.

"You're probably withdrawing from the Synth Gus, it's not gonna be roses."

The Synth, Synthetic Synergy, Pattern Powder, whatever, I use it sometimes, its for work actually, a couple people do, okay I suck it down every morning to start my day, and at noon to…keep it going. And then on weekends sporadically 'cause I bring work home sometimes.

"Well just give me a hit then."

"I can't Gus, this dude laid into you pretty hard, and from what I found out the Synth doesn't exactly mix well with head trauma."

He whispered which means no else knows I use, right? It doesn't show up in standard blood and piss tests, and the police probably thought my stash was an asthma inhaler like they were supposed to. If Martha found out I would seem deceptive, and the family—forget it, major disappointment. And the cops—the old order is so pissed off all the time they might throw the book at me, and I'd end up making motherboards in Rahway. The new cops, I don't know what they would do; send me to get "reeducated" or "treated" a couple-a-thousand miles away in United Free Timbuktu?

They don't know about the drugs. But I do, and boy do I need a hit.

I wanted to see myself with my hands like blind people do in movies. But when I raised my arms they felt so heavy and far away. When I reached my face Wyeth stepped back, from the squeak his sneaker made it seemed he nearly stumbled. My nose was bandaged, my hair gone (except for little random clumps which pulled out too easily), and below my ears (that were pounding like two throbbing hemorrhoids) were hard plastic tubes protruding from my flesh. Wyeth leaned into the bed, probably getting ready to stop me if I was to spaz out and remove what had been surgically implanted. I probed them with my fingers like people finger mysterious dents on their new cars. Inquisitive, heartbroken, angry. The tubes felt like the blue and red valves on the office water cooler, just a bit smaller.

"They're for relieving pressure, the nurse showed me how to use them. Sit still."

He was placing cold metal, could have been a bedpan, behind my neck. I felt the valve move a bit, then a gassy release and the sound of dripping water onto tin.

"There we go, easy as that."

My God, I wondered, what has happened to me? If only I had a little powder, just one quick inhale I could hold in and let the peace wash over me. Then maybe I could think straight.

A waft of perfume hit my nose. Only one of my nostrils was open but that odor was unmistakably female and sexy. It was my kind of girl, it was my girl, for sure it was Martha, and every cell of mine pulsed for her. It was out of control, literally out of my control, energy was surging and my breathing rushed.

A soft hand gripped mine; fear secreted from my skin. It turned me on. Was Wyeth in the room? I'm alone with Martha; she's climbing into bed. I am perfectly healthy and ready to shake off nightmares with mindless, thoughtless, loving sex—now! Oh, where has my libido been? Tied down by Synthetic Synergy, I'm guessing. Impotence is a minor side effect remedied by taking an over-the-counter pharmaceutical, of course. Do I want to take a hit of Synth or to grab this girl and release my tidal wave of masculinity? Is anyone else in the room?

"Gussy…"

Oh, my! She called me Gussy—so sexy. She wants it. Come here! The sheet rose between my legs. I blindly arched my back like something out of *The Exorcist*. Gripping her little hand, I reached with the other one and might even have exhaled a primal grunt. The burning hardness of it all shot straight upstairs to my head, and the new valves piped out foam and bubbles like a cappuccino machine on the fritz.

"*Huhhhh,*" she gasped, her voice streaming out like silk, and pulled away from me. Was there someone else in the room? What am I doing? She was crying, hugging someone. I've got to open my eyes!

No!

Drunken spins—faster than anything I remember. I try to put one foot on the floor. My twenty-first birthday, poisoned system with syrupy shots and cheap pitcher beer. The rotations are too much, too quick, can't keep up, got to open eyes.

Big mistake—unbelievably worse—seeing the world this way. The contorted images of two people with fat round heads and baseballs for eyes. The room had no corners and was melting into a collage of mixing colors and distant hospital sounds.

Beep, beep, nurse get me a…I love the flowers…It hurts…I'm scared…You'll be fine…let's see what it says on your chart….

All too much. The smell of sanitized floors and disposable clothing. Vomit coming up my guts and out my mouth, burning my throat, causing me to choke and cough. Erection so painfully hard, new openings spitting froth, death must be better. Large black man, hands like baseball mitts, sitting me up and turning my head, feet scuffling over floor, tears from Martha. Closing my eyes again, lights are dimming. This must be it.

*   *   *   *

I didn't have any visitors for a while after that. Within what seemed like a day of getting them, I had begun to get used to the pitch-black glasses. The shades were a gift from Wyeth, who apparently had been earnestly researching this side of my condition. The heavy visual hallucinations could continue for more than a week, than their potency would lessen dramatically. The duration of total withdrawal from Synth was different for every user. I would have been back on it if it wasn't for my immobility.

My energy was all over the place, even though I hadn't moved from the room. The powder could really take the edge off. It made me feel connected to life instead of a stranger. The world would be a better place if everyone took a hit off the old inhaler. Things would start running smooth. I took care of business when I felt peaceful—no distractions. Wyeth said it could cause an aneurism because of all the repair work that was going on in my brain. That's how Bruce Lee died, ya know.

*   *   *   *

The glasses weren't the only thing I was getting used to. I was comfortable enough with the cranial drainage system to start playing with it. By opening and closing each valve with a push of a finger, I could feel more in charge of my own health. I felt pressure build in my skull when they were closed for more than three hours and then got some sort of desperate pleasure from releasing a large quantity of frothy liquid all at once.

It wasn't too long before my family assembled around my sick bed. Their presence in the room felt charged with duty. Mom, Dad, Alexander my oldest brother, his wife and Uncle George accompanied by the police officers working the case all stood around, paced, and stared out the window into the parking lot until I was finally capable of holding a somewhat intelligible conversation. I told Wyeth to tell Martha I can't wait to see her, but just not now.

*   *   *   *

"This is my fault, buddy," were my brother's first words to me.

I have to admit I was surprised to hear the bigwig power broker. But his fault? What was that all about? I could just picture him standing there, with his slick hair and eyeballs that glistened from the special contact lenses he wore to protect him from so much screen time. The consummate businessman dressed in black: shiny shoes, slacks, computer-belt, and a crisp, tucked-in shirt. I'm sure he was wearing one of those medallions he loved to sport. Usually a silver geometric symbol was clipped to his collar which reflected his capitalist dogma and gave him the air of a dynamic New World priest. His faith was in the Free Market, and he did feed from its fruit generously.

"That motherfucker who did this to you!"

He was sounding sincere.

"*Aleco, stamata!*"

And being silenced by my mother—in Greek no less. He must really be feeling out of character now.

"Sorry Mom. Anyway, guy, the cops are gonna explain all this, but they hurt you to get to me. Labor union shit…."

"*Aleco!*"

"I know ma…."

"Alex—your tone—we're in a hospital." Penelope stepping in—big Alex getting it from all sides of the female front.

"Look, maybe it's not the time for this…I just want you to know…."

He was sincere, this is some serious shit, and to think I was worried they'd find my inhaler.

"I am sorry Gus. And…we're gonna do everything possible to get you healthy and back on track."

Then came the uncomfortable silence. I was pathetic wasn't I? Looking like Jason Voorheese in *Friday the 13th, Part 1*. Patchy head, paler than snow, busted up, beat down, drowning. Then I heard the praying and imagined everyone else reverently bowing their heads, hugging each other and sucking back pity tears while taking sneak peaks at the overexposed human catastrophe.

My mom's words were ancient. I couldn't understand them. Whispers. Scary feeling. Helpless. Small and shrinking fast. Disappearing in the darkness of my accidental life. Somebody say something.

Mom prayed a lot whenever Basil did a disappearing act, but she practically became a nun when Demetri enlisted. Demetri—the person you'd least expect to ever choose to carry a gun. His sympathy for others and his good heart actually made him a much-prized soldier of conviction, according to The Office of Expert Recruitment. Life is so sad. We need these strong bonds to survive in this world, and they are destined to be severed. It's only a matter of time until we all lose someone. My lips quivered and I was going to cry in the overwhelming tragedy of it all.

A little smooth piece of wood touched my forehead and calmed my face. Then the whispers became good, very good and real, and disaster was part of life. I knew the object on my skin to be an icon, a special holy thing. Suddenly hands were coming from all sides, and I was okay with it. In fact, I don't ever remember feeling so loved.

*   *   *   *

By sundown, when the room cooled and the outside sounds became nighttime ones, the room was once again empty. Flashbacks began to shock me out of my brief naps.

The kid was so quick, so efficient and ruthless. What kind of a world makes a monster like that? I was helpless, helpless now, hospitalized like a sick old person. I've got to get well, got to rebuild myself. The old man? He moved better then the Asian kid. He disappeared without the SAMs seeing him.

I meet the police tomorrow. After I hear their side I'm gonna make it my business to locate the old man and find out just how I ended up in this shitty situation.

CHAPTER 3

▼

SUNDAY NIGHT BLUES

Opium eaters
takers of pills
at the bar all day
blurry thrills
seems better than
panic
sober and awake
stomach ulcers sizzling
making mistake, after mistake, after mistake.
The bar man sits
cheating his sentence
the lucky old drunk
will never pay penance
and fall on his knees
and vomit out prayers
shake like a Shaker
with sweat in his hair
the world can't crush him down
when his elbows
are on the wood
a few inches of oak
and a bottle of blood

death doesn't bother
with outstanding men.

Time alone left me with the task of retracing the events that wound me up in this unhappy state. I remembered an average evening of watching television and escaping into someone's vision of entertainment. An image was being broadcast on our large-screen roll-up television. Martha and I sat together. Only the TV light illuminated the room. We were mushed into the soft, inflated couch and were locked into a horror movie, which glowed before us.

I could see her bare feet wriggling as if they were another entity sitting next to me. Martha's toenail paint was chipping in three spots, and on just one toe. She rubbed her right foot over her left a dozen times or more, but not more than twenty before switching feet and repeating the cycle. The movement brought out the faint smell of an aloe lotion she must have applied that evening. I can notice minutia if I choose to when I am full of Synth, and that night I was brimming with the stuff.

New accounts were given to me on Monday morning to work on for the month. I finished them in only a week. I was going to wait a while to notify my boss, though, didn't want to seem too efficient. But, what can I say? It was fun, I was riding on patterns of data while others were still hammering away at keyboards.

I chose to let my concentration be broken by a voice that came from the kitchen. "Change it! Please, I can't stay in here any longer, I've already eaten all your stuffed grape leaves, and I'm working on my fourth beer!"

The film we watched depicted a red hand sprouting obsidianlike black fingernails and holding what looked to be a unicorn's spiraled horn dipped in thick Indian ink. The limb that wrote was full of pumped up veins and sinewy muscle, while at the same time looked arthritic and pained. Bulbous knuckles appeared to be wrapped in the tight Hollywood skin of small-budget studio effects.

A letter was being written and the author narrated the document in creation. The monologue was delivered in a deep, spooky voice. Smoke-machine-looking vapors, like tiny cirrus clouds signaling coming weather, rose from below to mask the parchment. The grotesque pen moved in unison with the audible sentences. The words come out of my memory now as if from a broken machine, and I am conscious of them just before they are forgotten:

> Most hated lover, it is I Goro, Son of Hachiman—God of War, demonic royalty and great tactician in the battle against Yahweh. Goro

has rested long enough since the conversion of Constantine, Emperor of Rome. The day I whispered to him, "By this symbol you will lead,"

and showed him the vision of the cross, was a day Hell hath never forgot. In one moment of chicanery Goro began the destruction of the vile House-church, the Dormis-Ecclesia which threatened our hold on the green planet.

The narrator actually belched in disgust.

Eghhhh…martyrs and miscreants. Yes, by this symbol you will kill, rape, torture and enslave the world. How I lust Rome, and its continuous struggle for control. My brother forged Babylon, but I took its child and suckled it against your bleeding teat. I have watched Goro's work grow and flower into a hate filled world of deceived and frightful slaves. My father has busied himself lately in his great craft, and soon he will have the aid of his darkest, most fiery child.

So…speak to Lord Hachiman, and smooth my coming. There are those who still plot against my father. I sense the Prophet's movements, I know the Lightwalkers are rising, and Goro will rise as well! I will prove myself again in my father's sleepless eyes, I will strike down the enemy of Pure Hate. Goro orders the death of Constantine's soul!

The red hands rolled the parchment and held it up high. A great wind stirred up a dust storm and the prehistoric talons of an orange-skinned dragon snatched the rolled letter and disappeared in upward flight. Who writes this stuff? I momentarily wondered. And why do I watch it?

*   *   *   *

"It's over Wyeth, you can come in now, this bud has got you scareder than…" Martha paused before finishing her thought, having gotten equally as stoned as Wyeth on the super weed they'd bought in Brooklyn.

"More scared than a girl." Her sentence was completed but unexpected, even to her. It caused her to giggle uncontrollably, then abruptly stop and look around as if she didn't know where she was. "You and Gus can bond now, I'm tired." Her mind must have shoved back to the reality of my apartment in Queens New York.

Upon making her exit she caressed my ass on the sly. As Wyeth replaced Martha, I continued to stare into the screen. Wyeth picked up the remote and talked to himself as he changed the channel. His happiness in reuniting with the couch was apparent.

Goodbye Devil Channel 666, probably sponsored by the church of mullet-wearing America. Hello Martial Arts network! Wyeth really got into kung-fu flicks. Combined with quality marijuana and a fridge full of beer, he resembled Winnie the Pooh drunk on honey.

"Yes! Oh it's the end, who cares, this is awesome."

In my peripheral vision, his marshmallow stomach extended as he tilted his chin back for a big content chug. On the screen a Buddhist priest spoke in a blatantly dubbed voice about "Those who choose to serve God and man, with detachment and without hatred." Triumphant horns blared and the words KILLAH PRIEST appeared on the screen.

I mechanically rose and stabbed the power button with my fingertip. A split second whine emanated from the television, a hum of retracting power, then silence.

I spoke matter-of-factly. "Let's take care of that thing before Martha comes back."

Wye mechanically retrieved the plastic inhaler for me. It was in the shape of a nautilus and this month's color was purple. Sounding as wise as the kung fu movie's priest he told me, "Use it wisely Gus, this stuff ain't cheap, not to mention highly addictive."

I shoved it into my pocket and responded in my cool just-made-a-drug-deal voice.

"I know Wye, I'm weaning myself off now that I'm settling into the job."

That last word—job—turned his concerned look into a smile. I worked in a respectable field, and to Wyeth, it was like I was a made-man in the Mob or something. Since he was in my crew, he also had the respect in some roundabout way. He ended the night with nothing more to say except, "Goodnight Gus, I guess we both gotta work tomorrow."

The door closed behind my old college chum, and Martha's door opened to reveal her body's sparsely clad shadow. I knew this was going to be end-of-the-weekend sex, hard-working, desperate sex; I wish it wasn't Sunday-night sex. Martha, with her practical wisdom, had the Libidodex waiting on the night table, along with a glass of aerobically oxygenated bottled water. I swallowed the pills without a thought. Or at least what I thought wasn't a thought. Together we became one pulsating creature: humping, balled up, pumping, sweating, breathing hard and strong with hot life giving huffs into each other's holes.

*　　*　　*　　*

By 6am we were both up and sipping on an extreme sport drink, some extract from a jungle plant stimulant combined with rainbow dye No. 9.

"Honey," whispered Martha so as not to disturb the fragility of a Monday morning. "Let's not watch Channel 666 anymore. I had some really freaky dreams."

"No problem," I told her, "no more scary movies before bed." I comforted her with a logical solution, but I could not relate to her. At this time I didn't have bad dreams, or any real dreams for that matter. When I slept I went into the Dark Ocean. That's what users call it. I believe I was linking up with the pattern in my breathing. All I had to do was concentrate on making a few rhythmic breaths and Voila! I was there. The dark waters rose and receded, rose and receded, every night, just like that.

Synth is short for Synthetic Synergy. The hallucinogenic effect on the human brain allows the user to deeply connect with, and then creatively visualize what the sensory nervous system chooses to experience. This drug I had been inhaling for several months had stifled my ability to have dreams borne from my subconscious. The powder also affected my physical urges. I was rarely unnecessarily hungry, violent, or…horny. I didn't think about sex until I chose to, but when I did, let's just say, much like work, I was very effective. The high-grade Libidodex Martha would score from her Dad's medicine cabinet balanced out my libidinal deficit, and in fact made me a temporary sexual guru with all passion compartmentalized into the preplanned event.

Synth made working in a virtual medium easy and productive, and the rest of life content. I guess I could say that, when high, life is a good dream where invisible strings somehow connect all things, and I—I am in the center holding it all together by the very act of perceiving.

Because this narcotic enhanced my ability to experience patterns, and I had the desire and knowledge to apply it correctly, I became extremely valuable in Corporate America's new world of virtual-reality Generation 7 Language programmers. A data revolution had occurred recently which was driven by inevitable advances in hardware. Wearing eyepieces and using sensitive pieces of bio-circuitry, a new army of Data Harvesters was increasing commerce's productivity dramatically. A lot of us used Synth, and a lot of blind eyes were turned. I was high during my job interview. The cost-benefit analysis justified this sort of behavior because everybody in the business knew that a single Synth-fueled 7GL Harvester was worth a dozen traditional code-crunchers.

Martha put down her beverage and gave me a last sighing embrace before the waking world fell fully upon us both. We never talked about what was in my inhaler. She just accepted me for what I was. Maybe she absorbed some of the drug from my skin and everything was just part of the pattern, maybe she really didn't know I was a user because she never knew me any other way, or maybe…maybe she just didn't care because we didn't have the same problems that a lot of couples run into, and a well-kept castle could afford a dark, dirty dungeon.

I was silent; holding my lover in one arm, the drink in the other, I secretly toasted my own kingdom and my beloved queen. Would things have been different if I was still a computer peon? Absolutely. We probably wouldn't have ever met if I hadn't moved into this trendy neighborhood. Our block didn't have doormen, but it didn't have crime either, and that, along with convenient trains into Manhattan, made rents some of the highest in the five boroughs. We had lawyers in our building, and robot mechanics like Wyeth, and even a college professor who had his own studio. I dismissed thoughts of alternate futures and what-if questions. It was the moment that mattered, and that is what I lived in.

As king, the apartment's bedroom was my domain. Staring out onto the white wall my eyes rested upon a break in the pattern of things. Basil's wrinkled postcard was the anomaly. It hung tacked next to my bed and showed a landscape of red earth interspersed by twisty, dry-looking trees and lime-green brush. I reached out for my journal. The sun was preparing to rise over canyon country somewhere in the Utah high desert.

CHAPTER 4

▼

THROUGH THE LOOKING HAT

Spider webs
surround the earth
and carry deepest confidence
no one hears the first call
the signal beeping
S.O.S.
Pictures float
and voices mingle
onto screens
and into ears
the Hopi heard the eerie signal
before the spider web was here.
Transcribe the clicking
decipher a simple code
the skies grow redder
the webbing grows,
Making room for merchant's data
holograms are next
five thousand clicking
TV channels
android servants

will not
relay
S.O.S.

I drifted away from the sweat-soaked bed sheets and painful medical apparatus that were keeping me alive. I floated without distraction long enough to remember. Within memory I searched for reasons, and hoped that what I might find would give me direction.

* * * *

The city-bound N train, still sparse with passengers save but a few traveling from Queens, rattled and rocked me into mentally balancing my life's checkbook of achievements. I had finally become an achiever now, where formerly I was a waiter. Not a restaurant waiter, my parents would have liked that a lot more than what I was. I was in the waiting room of my post-college experience, so to speak. A do-nothing guy, a relaxed thinker, the type of slow-moving philosopher that capitalism dreaded: that was me. In my pajamas, at 10:30 AM every day, I rationalized my existence existentially over a cup of coffee at my parents' kitchen table. It was a peaceful, self-absorbed time.

Not anymore. Something clicked; I realized that while I was reading about being a free thinker, and getting high on the thought that the world was absurd, others were running the show and basically enslaving me. My cud fell out of my mouth in a green plop, and my sweet, milky coffee became sour.

The masters of this absurd reality were shunning me as a penniless lay-about, and suddenly I knew that I had to wait in line while they played the game. With lesser intellectual skills and far less mental self-sacrifice, the sheep were taking over and imposing their culture of ignorance on everyone who would not resist. I wanted more, and my Will to Power began. I put away my tattered notebooks, shelved the great works, and made data manipulation my study.

My plan had eventually worked and I achieved success. My first real success—ever.

* * * *

High school memories were almost completely erased and reformatted in order to deal with the letdown of the illusion of freedom that the adult world was supposed to offer. College had its challenges and minor achievements, but most were invisible battles of the mind. I feel now, in retrospect, that the study of philosophy, and the search for truth through Byronic heroism (excessive partying) were partially to blame for leaving my initial post-college ambition...purposeless.

The conversations went on too late and the "realizations" became too circular. The truth always bobbed in the waters that I searched through in the same form. The world was pure when one pursued purity, but, there was always another goal to reach, or more money to save up, before this golden path could be followed.

My reflections on my way to work were sidetracked by the presence that sat before me. Directly across from me was an old man in a tattered suit wearing a round, weathered hat on his head. The hat could have been a hundred years old. The rest of his wardrobe looked sewn together from several different decades. The man sharing my commute had a large skeleton, his skin was weathered and thin enough to reveal blue veins, which climbed from his temples into his covered, bald head. His hands were perched atop a cane. Looking at him reminded me of an old black-and-white photo I had once seen. The elderly gentleman smiled a happy, homeless smile that refreshed me like a seasonal breeze stealing its way through the metallic train doors.

The same small spark that tickled me into taking the time to journal my thoughts also created a click of blue light, deep in the recesses of my uncorrupted memory, that secretly illuminated to me the old man's great worth. To be free, to not have to work, or take drugs that made you work better was freedom. The world had changed, and the old homelessness seemed to be disappearing. To not pay into the System meant that you were essentially unbalancing the System. Relocation through government programs like "Project Fresh Start" was making old men like this into turn-of-the-century ghosts.

I analyzed my own place in life, including the order of my birth as the third of four boys. No longer was I afraid to measure myself against my siblings' worth. I was now on the charts. Oh, certainly not yet able to hold a candle to my eldest brother's extreme monetary success, nor could I begin to measure my own honor against younger Demetri's military rank and service. But certainly now I was self-reliant, and not bearing any of the guilt of anyone else's burden. The illumination of idealism flickered out in the vacuum of my own pride. I was a taxpayer now, and although all men are created equal, I gave in to feeling deserving of all the rights and privileges of a so-called good citizen. I never needed programs, or counseling, or therapy. I never had to go away to find myself, or whatever my missing brother had done. I know its wrong, but I still let the immature thought of me doing better than others, including Basil, wash over me and allow me brief, cowardly contentment.

The large, smiling person across from me exposed his own status through a two-inch long tear in his beat-up brown shoe. His big toe danced up and down and poked about from time to time. The black nylon sock gave the digit the appearance of a miniature puppet.

The worn shoes brought back more colorful memories of my brother. He was just nineteen when he came home from one of his earliest adventures in self-discovery. Six months on the trails and roads left him with a weather-beaten backpack, shabby clothes and a nappy head. He was lean, and fine wisps of facial hair that seemed to deposit themselves in a bunch on his chin drew his hollow cheekbones into looking even more gaunt. He must have neglected oral hygiene, because every time he smiled, which was often, he became more accurately medieval, or even biblical or prehistoric, by the looks of his brown and yellow teeth. He found a happiness out there, and the paranoia of destruction slept. His nomadic joy could not thrive in our static home.

While I, Demetrios, and our mother were regaled and taken aback by his stories of spiritual wellsprings and outrageous out-of-body ideas, our dad and eldest brother, Alexander, just ate dinner and nodded at him. As he shared his wonder with us they watched TV and looked at him only indirectly, or simply walked away; for the sight of their own blood rediscovering earthy, vagabond ways of thinking clearly disgusted them both.

The two eldest males in our nuclear family could only hope for change. Basil was beyond instruction in the ways of the Machiavellian world. They did have faith, though, that life itself, coarse and patient, would eventually wear down the purest of transcendentalists and conform to conventional decorum even the most faithful of backwoods Christians.

I thought to myself, if this homeless man sitting in front of me gets off at my stop I would like to buy him a cup of coffee at Slave to the Grind. The Grind provided me with a cup every weekday morning, and was a way of rewarding myself for making it to my midtown office with a half hour to spare. The shop was a positive environment where customers' moods seemed of primary importance to the establishment. As a user of Synthetic Synergy, I appreciated a place that could jump-start my high in the morning.

My focus shifted from self-analysis, and I began to watch a teenage girl who wore extremely baggy clothing. She moved a carriage back and forth and tried to lull her crying child by matching the train's rocking rhythm. I imagined this young mother caught up by a great wind and floating easily, escaping her day-to-day problems. Holding her child's hand, she would hover above the city and return to her grandparents' native land.

I began to see the connectivity in the immediate world around my self. The Synth was kicking in right on time and everyone was engaged in the pattern. A young Asian man was trance dancing. Wearing old-school headphones, his body moved in a small space and had the fluidity of liquid. His hands cradled an invisible and dynamic ball of energy. A middle-aged white male began handing out flyers and announcing something that caused a jarring ripple in the otherwise mundane journey.

"Do not accept the mark of the beast!"

A SAMURAI began to move toward the ripple. The SAM cop's presence was nearly undetectable before he reacted. He had previously been standing totally still against the train's door.

A series of almost imperceptible movements left the would-be religious radical in zip-tie cuffs and unable to speak due to the pressure-point hold the cop applied just below the man's rib cage. The deviant appeared to be in pain and mouthed a silent scream. The officer addressed the car in slow second-language English:

"Bleaze excuse dis man fo disturbing yo ride to werk, dare are proper forums to express one's views to da public."

This SAM was a dark African with thin Oriental eyes. SAMURAI were no longer an experiment in New York City. Their high number of arrests and non-lethal takedowns had made them popular. They came from all over the United Free World, and had all served in the United Nation's Secular Army Police Force.

The SAMs were the next logical step after the Gun Ban started to work. "Strict Legislation/Electronic Detection" was the mayor's borrowed slogan for a safe city. The NYPD was being gradually retired and moved into the high-paying private sector while the SAMURAI held the city's new banner of safety and success. These New World cops brought hope from foreign cities that had been made secure. Guns had been efficiently and systematically confiscated and destroyed; the penalty for possession was harsh. One could feel a sense of safety when a SAM, usually accompanied by a robotic canine (a gun-sniffer) came on the scene.

SAMURAI were typically unarmed, although rumor had it that the gloves they wore could deliver an electric shock strong enough to cause unconsciousness. They were always potentially lethal, with or without arms, for their bodies were trained weapons. Their extreme training in martial arts sounded nothing short of mythical. The cops were becoming heroes in black, flexible body armor who were already worthy of a weekly TV drama based loosely on real characters. The Secular Army was the brainchild of the UN. With so much religious conflict in the world, this group was welcomed as the guardians of pure, objective, democratic law.

The SAMURAI dogs were specifically designed to read the presence of firearms, ammunition, and explosives. Their noses were advanced chemical-detecting devices, while their mouths emitted a sonar bark that received back X-ray images of objects to be instantly cross-referenced with blueprints on their hard drives. Once illegal material was acknowledged, a signal was sent out and the photographic eyes of the dog went to work on preparing a task force, if necessary, to move in on the subway car, apartment building, concert hall, or anywhere that needed action. Cartoons, comics, and video games about SAMURAI held the affection of children and adults worldwide.

The train halted at its assigned stop, and the now-silent officer exited with his prisoner as quickly and quietly as he had apprehended him. "Miranda" was not a word the internationally-affiliated police knew very well. The teenage mother exited behind the small crime drama. I searched for the pattern again and found it in the consistent flowing movement of the trance-dancer.

The kid was moving like someone at a retro rave party. The liquid kid reminded me of Wyeth. It's not like Neederman could dance, mind you; he has serious trouble putting on his socks while standing. I thought of Neederman because he never cared who was looking. He just did things, and I often got embarrassed for him. Wyeth was the one who encouraged me to try out for the Data Harvester training program even though I was hesitant because of my lack of experience. He said, as he usually did, "Who cares, fuck it, if it doesn't work out we'll have a beer for tryin." Somehow I made the cut and he didn't; I'm a BDH (Bonded Data Harvester), and he helps fix remote-operated vacuums. Who cares, the beers are on me, now.

The dancer's movements were definitely revealing themselves as those of a practiced student of a physical art. His actions became cleaner, and his fingers left trails as they raked the air. I stared hypnotically and wished the performance could go on forever.

"I carry a picture of you wherever I go," the old man leaned over and told me in a very refined almost British accent. I smiled, pulled myself away from the show, and noticed that the gentleman speaking to me lacked eyebrows. Perhaps cancer? Regardless of the pattern I was missing, I knew that in the past, many a quirky passenger had made my subway journey an entertaining one.

"Are you British?" I naively asked. "I notice you have an accent." (Assuming my powers of perception were accurate.)

"No young man, you are simply not regularly in contact with people who think before they speak. Proper etiquette is the cornerstone of a gentleman's character. And although I do have fond memories of all my visits to the British Isles, New Jersey happens to be my place of birth."

The response from the man without hair bordered on sounding pompous. Fearing I had offended the stranger, I immediately replied to fill any discomfort that a lull in conversation might hold. "I'm from New Jersey, too."

The man smiled long with thin, leathery lips, his teeth not yet revealed. "I carry a picture of you wherever I go," he told me a second time.

I realized I was hearing the same thing again and understood that it must be important in this man's perhaps warped mind. "Is that right? Ok, let's see it." Least I could do was entertain his fantasy, and who knows, maybe I'd get a cool visual out of it.

The dignified character straightened his spine, and gripped the back of his once fine hat with his right hand. The head-cover seemed to gently roll in a perfect series of turns down his long arm and through the air, ending with the inside top six inches from my eyes. A round mirror, secured into his hat, had me staring directly into my own eyes. There was no escaping, no witty comment to change this situation. I began to look at myself in that brief moment without the justifying eyes of an analyst. I saw myself, was forced out of my mind's image of who I was, and felt scared.

Green eyes revealed the drug that had helped me lie and cheat my way into a life I may never really have wanted, into a new status, into an apartment and into Martha Walpole's bed. The gel I rubbed into my short hair, combined with a raw-shaven, ashen face, made me glisten with an aura of the unauthentic—phony, and not real. I felt terrible, seasick, like waking from a drunken blackout. Then the mirror was gone, and the hat back on its owner's head. The man in tan smiled; a big, strong, gray-toothed smile.

The screech of the train came, doors sucked open, commotion of transferring workers trying to make it on time. The old guy disappeared. I began an internal coaching of myself.

Shake it off. Get to work and plug into the System, make these guys some money and earn your pay, the old fashioned way. Like dad did engineering, being a part of the creation of things, chemical plants that take the caffeine out of coffee and the salt out of seawater. You're just having an exceptionally weird morning.

We sell data at the Creel Corporation; quantities of socks from Singapore, weight of sugar from Brazil. I am fortunate enough to be able to bond with one of the largest databases on the planet and extract information for the salesmen on my floor in a timely and efficient manner. I am working hard; what would a homeless old phony Britisher know about that?

*   *   *   *

Recalling those events that unfolded just prior to my becoming a victim gave me a mission. With my brother's personal investigator's help, and the cooperation of the police, the subway's digital cameras were accessed and the roster of homeless men was profiled. My hero was William Ringle, originally from New Jersey, now residing in several shelters around the city. The only real address he could now be connected with was in Morningside Heights, in Harlem. William Ringle's brother, Thomas, was all I had to go with now.

Meanwhile, I couldn't see, couldn't control embarrassing libidinal surges, and never really slept. The injuries were painful, and the withdrawal process was only just beginning. Still, I was checking out in two days and moving back in with Wyeth. Saturday couldn't come soon enough for me. I looked forward to being mobile again, and wondered what Tommy Ringle would be like.

CHAPTER 5

▼

THINGS GREATER THAN TAI CHI

There is no finer hour
than dawn
even in an arid place
of car traffic, without shade.
The early morn is serene,
cool, a dreamy painting
where people can meet without masks
with special personalities
that movies have difficulty imitating or capturing.
It's the smiles I think,
goofy, like jack-o-lanterns
they spread on the faces of
waitresses and coffee slurpers
unconsciously, without effort.
The Tai Chi of the red and orange horizon
paints itself without motivation.
It is the film about catastrophe
that leaves great streets empty.

Martha raised her arms and pulled both curtains open at once, revealing Saturday Morning sunlight. I glimpsed the world in darkened blinks, not trusting my eyes. I noticed the aloe vera plant below the sill looked green and healthy, fat with the eastern light that strikes it first thing in the morning.

She put music on, ambient weird stuff. Different, but gentle. Soothing me, my skeleton relaxing. The muscles of my face dropped. I exhaled, and breathed in a soft smoky scent. Incense. Martha was taking care of me. I love her, I think.

An ethereal rising happened. I almost cried from some sort of sad joy. My nose felt wet and if I tried to speak I knew my words would crack and I would blubber, so I stayed still, and continued to rise, inside, my soul maybe. There was ecstasy in this loose concentration on the music, and the smell, and the breeze, and…she touched me. Massaged my temples with fingers just strong enough. Her skin was cooler than mine and felt like a goddess's. A female deity healing me, with her lips pressed against my forehead.

"You're going to take these off Gussy."

My dark glasses. She commanded me to remove them. I would do so, albeit carefully, and as if they were melted onto my skin, my deliberate hands would ensure that my mask-of-a-face wouldn't be removed as well. Her just-right palms moved over the Frankenstein scars, then navigated my shoulders and finished at my fingers. She cupped them and directed the removal of my own grim eye ware.

I could see. The little world inside of our Queens, New York kitchen was beautiful. My lover was standing before me like a work of art, as if she had been made perfect by my illness. Innocent but ancient. A soul wrapped in soft skin, peering out through caring eyes. *This must be the balance*, I might have said lightly. Or thought it. *The good part about withdrawing from the Pattern Powder.*

"Gus, you can really see me?" Martha asked with tears in her voice.

"Yeah, and what a relief, you look so good, so pretty today."

She was struck by my words. She'd been through a lot, also, since Tada came for me. The stress to her life and the terror of the situation must have put her will to the test. What if he killed me? Would my girlfriend mourn like a widow? I'm sure she had to face those kinds of imaginings while staring at my comatose shell.

I folded the glasses; she placed them on the counter. I parted her brown sugar hair, and like curtains opening she smiled. The speckles around her irises danced in small planets of brown glass.

Words were scarce for both of us. She kissed me, and my dry mouth moistened under the touch of her lips. Gently, she pushed off my lap and stood. I gazed up like a virgin in a whorehouse, in awe of her body's curves. She was changing the music. Something bright, raspy, and very American came on.

This is why they do it, I thought. *Why we really marry.* This, this, union, this promise of life together forever, seemed so right. I wanted to tell her, hold her, and make her know that I knew this meaning of life. I wanted to do so much else when it all abruptly fell apart and my world retreated back to the twisted illusion of Synergy withdrawal.

Wyeth had unlocked the front door and let it slam against the wall, jarring my reverie. I could handle not using, dealing with all life's day-to-day shit and always awaiting the brief splendid moments of feeling alive. I could deal with sobriety, and stoically endure, and forever be learning from the monkey on my back if...if it wasn't for the damn hallucinations. When the madness took over, one hit could bring me back, one hit could end it. One hit could kill me.

"I'm home my friends!" was Wyeth's innocently destructive greeting. He turned the TV on, as he habitually does when he stomps in. Something flipped when my concentration shifted. My romantic vision faded as if it were as fragile as a ring of smoke.

The kitchen became a nautilus in lavalike motion. The walls turned to a hot gel that burned at my sanity. The TV screen, dead and blank a minute ago, shined now with villainous energy. A red demon looking into a bowl of water as if it were a future-telling device stared up from his own painful hideous face and roared out my name like a hot breathed grizzly, "Cone-Stan-Tine!"

My hands sprang to cover my vision; I fell to my knees and tightened up all over. *Will not give in...will not give in!* became my struggling mantra. Feet slid in to assist me, then stopped. It was my time and they were good enough friends to know my recovery belonged to me. I rose to one shaky knee. *Will not....*

Thought I heard Martha's teardrop explode against the floor. Someone turned off the television. My will pushed me to stand. Sometimes all a person needs is a little space.

"Hand me the glasses."

Everybody exhaled.

"You got it Gus!" Wye was psyched up by my underdog show.

Martha, too, was ready for this chapter to end. "Now go find your Mr. Ringle," she said.

*   *   *   *

Without sight, the train was full of sounds and smells that grossed me out. When not calming down my pounding heart and wiping the sweat from my closed eyes, I fought waves of nausea. The train was a worm and I was in its gizzard, churning with the rest of the earth.

Wyeth held my arm and told me we'd be there soon enough. Harlem smelled spicy and alive. The sidewalk was crowded but we didn't bump into anyone. I guessed the crowd pitied a blind guy and instinctively moved out of our way. My seeing-eye human was focused on the address, while I wondered if the person would match the polite voice on the phone. I only opened my eyes to take quick peeks at the world. Fear of my brain distorting visual images kept me mostly in the dark.

Ringle was across from his apartment building this afternoon. Wyeth explained that he was teaching beneath stone monoliths of wealthy Dutchmen, surrounded by a crowd of students observing his unique form of martial exercise. The Nei Kung class he instructed was ending as we got there and the twenty-some practitioners attending were sounding peaceful and kind to each other in departing, as if they had found a place to regenerate themselves in the tumult of the ever-raging city.

"Thank you Sifu, Thank you Sifu," was what I kept hearing. Wyeth whispered to me that the departing students had bowed with an open hand covering a closed fist. When the crowd was gone, Sifu Tommy stood still and smiled. Wyeth described him as a little guy in sweatpants and baggy T-shirt.

When everyone had gone Sifu Tommy stood still and let his arms hang at his sides. I took a split second snapshot. His pose gave him a childlike appearance. With a straight back and a motionless head, he met the sunlight like a flower.

"He could have been a blind guy himself," Wyeth later said, "the way he stood, all motionless."

A few more steps and another snap shot. An oversized Yankees cap hid his face and eyes, but as we entered his space the small voice said, "I am sorry for what that boy did to you." The words sounded teary and honestly sad. "Walk with me, behind this tree."

Wyeth reacted protectively, "Whoa, Mr. Ringle, look, I brought Gus here to maybe meet your brother, give the guy some closure...you know."

I had to interrupt my friend's sensible comment because I had a feeling about something, and when you're blind for a while, you start to trust such things. "It's okay Wye, I'd love to take a walk with you...Sifu."

Ringle took me by the elbow, like a small child tugging on a parent to show them something amazing in a museum. I reached out and recognized that we had stopped under a large sycamore. Its trunk was as wide as I was tall. He removed my glasses and dropped them in the grass.

32   Naked Among the Tombs

"I want to give you something," were Tommy's words. With more hope than fear I watched as he held his palms up as if balancing two cups of tea in front of my face.

I would come to understand this later as serving *chi*. The invisible cups were held by fingers with untrimmed nails that appeared like little rivers, frozen in their swirling motion. Next he stepped back and dropped into a stance with his left foot leading, palms together in a prayerful, yet martial way. The palms separated and the right palm moved forward and lightly settled on my sternum. Closing my eyes again I could hear the leaves rustle above me, and felt a pleasant heat through my shirt. The tree, the earth, felt so inviting at that moment, so welcoming of their injured guest.

The moment? How long have I been standing here? It feels like a thousand years, a wonderful millennia spent in prayer just standing here. This is what I was thinking before I got healed.

"Can you see me now? You can't see me with your eyes closed, he, he, he, he, he."

He was giggling. Tommy's words and laughter pulled me from reverie and into a seemingly miraculous surprise. His smile was the first thing I clearly saw, it was wide and goofy. His features hinted at Down's syndrome. His age was difficult even to estimate. His innocence was blaringly obvious.

This man healed me, or at least facilitated the fix somehow. My body felt fantastic, like I had removed an iron suit. It was beautiful in its motions and design. Dramatic as it may sound, the simple wonder of my life was blowing me away. All the bones in my hands opening and closing and my lungs expanding and contracting made me feel loved by the forces around me, and I felt in love with the idea of eternal life.

*   *   *   *

Ringle walked away then and I knew not to follow. He left to complete the circle and finish the balance.

I greeted Wyeth with a hug and a new found awareness.

"Holy shit! Gus! You okay?" was his question in between puffs on a cigarette.

"Be a good lad and loan an old man one of those fags," spoke a mysterious regal voice.

It was who we were looking for, Tommy's brother, the man from the train with the old hat and quick feet. What a day! I thought.

"What the fuck?" Wyeth whispered.

Looking my way, William Ringle said, "My brother is resting now. Perhaps you have some questions for me?" Tipping his hat at Wyeth, he said with a smile, "Perhaps you'll buy us some coffee?"

The shop we walked to also baked bread. The olfactory stimulation was making my reborn senses high. The place was not generic. It was open, jazzy, and very Harlem. A smoke-easy establishment, where customers could feel as cool as a movie star lighting up in a motion picture. The screen door bounced twice after Wyeth entered. The old man had no money, and Wye jammed a hand into his own pocket before sitting. He fingered bills and I guessed he was also double-checking his pot stash for the day.

All of my nose sniffed away and searched for the perfect scent. My eyes danced from image to colorful image. A child stole through the kitchen playfully wearing oversized ski gloves. Jazz layered the room and conversations circulated in the atmosphere.

Neederman began with what I'd told him had happened on the subway. "Why did you stay to help when everyone else fled, like we learn to do on TV?"

"I don't watch TV, m'boy. You should really try the scones here. May I have a light?"

My turn. "Why did you show me...myself...on the train?" I asked quickly, too quickly I realized, without giving it enough thought.

William Ringle's head smoothed out as he exhaled, its sun blotched coloration reminded me of the Sycamore's bark. He responded to my hasty question, "Well, if I did that, it must be a good thing, so why question a gift? Isn't the answer a question, and isn't that question, Is a true gift something good?"

Again, with haste, not waiting long enough to even be puzzled, I fired out another one. "Did your brother just take away my injuries?"

Another inhale, then he answered matter-of-factly, "No, he assisted your body in realigning itself with the universe. Improved health is just a minor side effect."

Neederman was skeptical. I knew he was looking at this man as another one of New York's perhaps interesting, and even, if circumstance has it, good-Samaritan residents who happen, however, to be mentally ill.

I contemplated the old man's words and they circled my head like ancient maxims. I felt comfortable asking the questions I really wanted answers to. "Why do you live in the shelters? Where did you learn how to fight? And how can I learn?"

To my thankful surprise, he responded without sign of awkwardness or intrusion.

"I am a Taoist, and in this temperate weather I sleep out of doors. Tommy and I grew up in China and were fortunate to receive fine educations. He took to Tai Chi practice at an early age as recommended by our family's physician. Not only to improve his health but in following a natural aptitude for the martial arts."

Hearing William Ringle say these things made Wyeth raise an eyebrow in a gesture of mocking disbelief.

William continued. "He was allowed to become a live-in student in the great temple, with our father's permission, of course, and practiced ceaselessly while I filled my days less with boxing and more with theatre, and sometimes...magic."

The coffees came, and I smiled confidently that my stomach's constitution would match the rest of my body's new-found strength. The aromatic cup would be the first taste of the black bean since the morning of the beating.

"Tommy will not train you however, and never in the fighting arts. The students in this morning's class are all teachers of the martial arts themselves, and have earned Tommy's instruction with many patient years of waiting."

"Can you teach me William?" It just came out. "You obviously move pretty good."

The old man put his cup down and met my eyes with his, an air of seriousness followed. "You must rebuild now. Your body, mind, and most importantly, your spirit."

"Did my attacker take that much from me?"

William replied kindly, "No my boy, this world did."

A pause settled on our table. William took advantage of it by closing his eyes and allowing a breeze to caress his scalp. He spoke again when the breeze finished its work. "Lust for revenge may grow too strong; guard against it. Fear must not guide your training. It is not a good intent. I can offer you my friendship, though."

From the kitchen, wearing an apron, a woman approached our meeting. Her black hair was pulled back and she smoothed out her skirt with both hands. Seemingly hurried and in the middle of work, she addressed William. "Mister Ringle. I was hoping you were here today. Santo and his cousins just love when you talk with them."

William had stood and his large hand invited her small dough-sticky fingers. Her stress melted with William's touch and her voice came more down to earth. "Oh, you are so kind. I just don't know what to do sometimes."

"My lady, the children await."

She apologized to Wyeth and me, and led the way, still holding on to Ringle. We followed curiously; passed customers, moved around bread ovens, and entered into a small back room. Santo still had the ski gloves on and was chasing three other kids in a game of tag.

"SAMURAI cop gonna shock you out!" Santo yelled as he collided with his mother's apron. The other three screamed like prepubescent banshees. One stood on a card table and was reaching for a grip that didn't exist on the smooth wall. Another hid beneath the table, another was behind me holding my leg with a small, sharp grip.

"Santo! *Mira*! Mister Ringle is here and I think he might have a story for you."

The little brown-skinned boy stopped cold and let his heavy hands fall to his sides.

"Santo, boys, it is so nice to see you today," William squatted to their eye level when he spoke.

The boys helped Santo by pulling the gloves off and flinging them to the floor. The climber's death-defying leap landed him with both sneakers touching down next to the gloves. They raced to sit cross-legged and formed a semi circle, then looked each other over to make sure everyone was on board. The hard-working mother took William's hand in both of hers and whispered, "Thank you."

"Those loaves await your magic touch my dear. My friends will join us?"

"Of course, hi guys, make yourselves at home."

Wyeth and I joined the eager audience.

William removed his shoes, jacket, and hat; his cane hung from the doorknob. He asked the children if they had been watching the sky at night from their rooftops. They answered affirmatively, and as if they each had found something in their observations that no one had ever seen before.

"How did the night sky come to be?" William asked, and I had to remind myself that this question was for the children, and I felt embarrassed for almost blurting an answer.

"It just is," said Santo confidently.

Smiling proudly, William honored the boy's answer with patient silence before replying, "Correct my boy, it just is. This story is about how it came to be before it just was."

Smiles and tight stomached looks of eagerness let me know the story was about to unfold.

"There was a time, before this time, when darkness was not strong, and only lived deep inside of caves." William's arms directed us upward and the permanent sunlight of imagination warmed the room.

"The people and the animals and the insects all spoke the same language, and danced in the magic sunlight and lived in dreamtime and never needed to sleep. All the beings danced and sang in the great circle, leaving only to snack on the fruits of the earth.

"One day, the people left the great circle for food but did not return. The other creatures worried and sang songs loudly so that if the people were lost they could hear the song and find their way. But the people were not lost at all, they had found the great cave, and fallen in love with the darkness."

William shrank, kneeling and bending into a hunched position. The children gently gasped.

"In the darkness they found special games and mysteries that no other creature could know, and even though they grew lonely, would not share with any one. Soon, they stopped sharing the games with each other, and sat alone, in cold damp places, playing the games and holding the mysteries that were too good to share with others.

"When snack time came, though, the cave was without food. So after wandering out into the bright sunlight for fruit, the first person shouted in pain for the light burnt his eyes very badly! His eyes felt like salty water was poured inside and tears filled his cheeks. Before running back inside, he looked up with a hand covering his view and shouted, 'I hate the light!'

"His shout was so loud and his word so strong that the creatures, for just a minute, stopped dancing. They listened to the silence and were sad."

William illustrated his narration with histrionics, and was the most supple, fluid thespian I have ever witnessed.

"Their usual joy, however, was interrupted but again, by a great booming voice no creature had ever heard before:

'YOU DARE TO SPEAK BADLY OF THE WONDERFUL LIGHT THAT GIVES YOU FRUIT!'" William boomed like thunder and rose on his toes to be even taller than he was. We all stared up in amazement.

"'FOR WHAT YOU HAVE DONE, I WILL TAKE AWAY THE LIGHT!'

"Then the voice rolled a great black cloth across the sky, and the light shone down no more. All the creatures fell down and were scared. Even the people were frozen with fear, and huddled together and cried. The creatures missed the light, and began to plan how to get it back.

"The first one to speak was Alley Cat. 'I am the quickest creature in the land, and I will fix this mess!' All the animals cheered for Alley Cat as he ran with all his might, and climbed the tallest place. The brave cat leapt with courage and hooked his claws into the great black cloth. Just then, a mighty ripping sound tore across the sky, for Cat's claws were not fingers and could not hold the cloth. He plummeted to earth. With a crash he hit. The animals looked up and saw that his claws poked holes in the shape of a great spoon that dipped out light. Cat dusted himself off and cried, 'Who's next?'

"Pit Bull stepped up. 'I can do it!' And the biggest, roughest pit bull ran and ran back up the highpoint. She leapt from the top, and bam! Her head poked through the cloth and the animals cheered 'Hooray!' But then they heard Pit screaming, her big head was on fire, she pushed off and fell to earth, fiery head and all. The raccoons came out and spit water on her head that they had carried in their mouths. And when she shook herself off, her head was a different color then her body for the light behind the cloth had singed her fur. She was even more mangy and mean looking then before! The children cracked up upon hearing that.

"And when she looked up, she saw the great hole her head made pouring out a wonderful brightness, and that is the Fullest Moon. She thanked the raccoons for their help and encouraged them to try. The little creatures used their special hands to climb on each others' shoulders, and soon made a raccoon ladder that touched the great cloth!"

William stood straight and began to teeter and bend.

"Just as the last little hand reached up and touched the cloth the ladder fell apart. On their way down they threw their arms to hold on and socked each other right in the eyes. On the earth they laughed, because they all had black eyes and looked as if they wore masks.

"Finally, Pigeons landed. 'We will do it,' they chirped. And all at once, they flew straight toward the cloth. They flew by the thousands, then by the millions, then no one could count all the wonderful pigeons filling the sky. They poked their beaks through the blackness and pulled and pulled but could not fly backward. One by one, they too hit the dirt. But when they looked up they realized they had made too many tiny holes to count. They called the holes The Stars, and laughed at the beauty they helped make.

"The cloth was full of holes and looked wonderful. Everyone looked up and was quiet. In the silence they heard a tiny voice, the voice of grandmother spider. 'When you were working so hard, I too was working. I have just finished weaving a giant web to the back of the creator's cloth, and now, I am ready to roll it up.' As carefully as she weaved it, she began to roll it up. And sure enough, the darkness began to disappear. The great cloth was gone, and the light shone on the earth again.

"Everyone rejoiced and said that Grandmother Spider was the wisest one of all. Even the people came out of the darkness and cried with joy, and rejoiced that the light had returned.

"But the dancing stopped...when the voice came back.

"'YOU HAVE DONE IT NOW! ROLLED UP MY CLOTH!'"

Everyone ran for cover, and hid from the voice.

"'I AM HAPPY. YOU HAVE WORKED TOGETHER, AND THE PEOPLE HAVE REALIZED THE BEAUTY THEY HAD LOST. FOR YOUR EFFORTS AND YOUR HARD LESSON, I WILL LET THE LIGHT SHINE AND CALL IT DAY, AND THEN I WILL UNROLL THE HOLY CLOTH, AND WE WILL CALL IT NIGHT.'"

"And that is how the night sky came to be."

*   *   *   *

Santo and his rough crew thanked us with handshakes and a fresh muffin each. We stayed a while and drank coffee, and I observed the customers coming in and out and talking into small phones and wondered if they were holding on to mysteries they found in the darkness. I stared into the swirl of my coffee and asked myself if the strange Tommy, brother of homeless William, actually healed me, or if maybe the drug had just run its course and my body finished its work.

I had been offered friendship from my remarkable and learned hero, and stubbornly thought more about pursuing lessons in the fighting arts. William explained to me: "Tai Chi is truly a blessed thing, and even though its very name means Supreme Ultimate, there are things in this world even greater than Tai Chi."

I felt so good and excited that stumbling blocks might really be stepping-stones to greater things. I imagined that the dark days, full of strange coincidence and potential miracle, were opening up a new world for me and were the beginning of some better life.

CHAPTER 6

▼

BACK TO THE GRIND

*One can sit
while traveling
and with practice, patience, and faith,
become a universal citizen.*

The office was beeping and spitting coffee from vending machines. My jaw ached, and I was chewing on things for the same reason someone might pick at a scab. The maze of cubicles seemed an illogical arrangement, the computer station I bonded with felt unnatural. The salesmen I supported appeared pathetic and insane.

To use the terminal's eyepiece I had to stare into it as if it were one of those hidden-picture cards, the kind where a number may appear within a blobby color scheme. 7GL programmers are trained to get lost in the scheme of pixels held just half an inch from one's iris. Once the comfort level is found, data can be harvested visually, and accessed with a gel mouse.

With this setup, I could transform data extraction into a walk through pastures and crop fields of information. I had the catalog of symbols memorized. Some data becomes virtual wheat bundles, or even livestock, and continually morphs before the gentle grasp of a good harvester. This virtual accessing of information takes all the coded calculation part out of database programming. Because the real work is behind the scenes, visual variables solely represent data to the harvester. Arranging the content in various complex scenarios, in comparison to the old way, takes place at an alarmingly fast pace.

The gel mouse is a gelatinous solution that was the first public use of non-medical biological circuitry; a living interface device. The harvester's hand rests in the bowl of non-stick goo and allows for a hundred times more grabbing power than the original mouse or touch pad.

The Synth had once made the gel mouse fun, almost magical in allowing me to "touch" information and store it in e-barns and have it processed in e-mills. Now my hand felt intrusive, perverse and in a place it did not belong. This was a far cry from when I began as an intern with the company, before I had the 7GL training. It was so different then, using the small programs that were a struggle to write. The old code had spoken to the machine in a language closer to binary. Once I became a 7GL programmer, the gel mated me with the machine, and "talking" was no longer necessary.

The rest of my body was free to use a phone and converse with the sales department, or anybody else, from any corner of the planet, who requested the high-priced information bundles that fueled the world's wheelings and dealings. The drug had made everything tolerable in the past, even the relentless requests from commission-hungry people like Brian Obermann. I overheard his pitch this morning and suddenly could not believe that it hadn't changed.

"Hello, this is Brian Obermann. I'm just calling to say hi and let you know that your interest in international trade has not been overlooked, and as the largest data warehouse on the planet, The Creel Corporation wants you to know that we are here to support your spirit of business adventure in this exciting global market..."

Some warm-up work was put on my desk by 9:00 AM. It was my first request from one of the five cubicles that surrounded my area in a panopticon. The sales team plugged away, and the queen in the middle produced. *Weight of copper mined in the continent of Africa.* The request for this data started from an up and coming chip company based in Egypt.

"Hello, this is Brian Obermann. I'm just calling to say 'hi' and let you know that your interest in international trade has not been overlooked, and as the largest data warehouse on the planet, The Creel Corporation wants you to know that we are here to support your spirit of business adventure in this exciting global market...."

The sales people didn't pull it off their user-friendly database page because the copper weight that needed to be concatenated with the annual weights from more than a dozen specific years had to exclude all copper mined in UFSA-occupied territories and needed to be delivered in a system of measurement only used by the Federation For Free Scientists of Democratic Monarchies (whose details were to be kept confidential, according to Creel's department of Client Rights).

I turned away from the written request and immediately pulled into the "year fields." I stared into the image used to represent the current year. If I could get past this symbol then I could enter the "farm." I peered into this picture and froze. Why was this happening? Why suddenly was I looking into an image of something sinister, red, and clearly representing evil instead of a plain normal lime-green variable? Why the demon mask? Oh no…what's happening? The eyes…they're fucking with me, scaring me, hypnotic…drawing me to join them, to wear this mask!

Seventh Generation Coding used dynamic symbols; they could change, according to the user's perception. If the harvester wanted to, and had the aptitude to work with complexity, then the variable would become unique and specific. The important part was recognizing similar patterns in data; then, the image would come not from the writer, but from the brain of, or rather from the hand and eye of the user as analyzed by algorithms—the hidden mathematics that made variables, which become symbols. This changing symbolism allowed more complex detail in data recall, and a very high volume for potential transport. Because of people like me, the database could be loaded continuously with information from millions of digital sources without expending resources on sorting and storing sorted data. I was the bright future, ya see—if I could figure out how to handle the present situation.

"Hello, this is Brian Obermann. I'm just calling to say hi and let you know that your interest in international trade has not been overlooked, and as the largest data warehouse on the planet, The Creel Corporation wants you to know that we are here to support your spirit of business adventure in this exciting global market.…"

I gasped and felt helpless enough to cry. My regression was upsetting, my loss of paradise intolerable. I squeezed that gel and tried to hold on. Exploding pixels lit up my eyepiece and rid me of the hellish obstacle. Tearing the black glob from its box I hurled it to my left and it found its mark on the back of Brian Obermann's shiny black head. He had been shaving it clean three mornings each week since graduating college. It was his statement, his "work head."

Splat! was the sound that accompanied the strike of the cold jellyfish like missile that now dripped into his collared shirt.

"What the fuck!" were the first words I had heard him speak besides his sales spiel in a very long time.

My wide-open shocked eyes could only stare at this fuming co-worker before me. And my mouth released the words, "Can you believe what year it is already!"

Mr. Obermann, the month of March's biggest seller, did not feel respected. With a "You mother fu...!" he charged me and I ran scared.

My shoulders rubbed against the light blue cubicle walls. The static electricity caused by my shirt fueled my escape energy. I stole into the bathroom and locked myself behind the first open stall. Obermann's shoes slid in like Fred Astaire's. There was another sound then, someone else had entered just behind Obermann.

"Whoa, what's all the excitement about Bri? Gonna shit yourself or somethin'?"

This question made me think of my own sorry intestinal condition. I didn't mention this, but I haven't had a peristaltic movement in several days. In the past, the drug, the Synth, had taken care of my regularity. Every morning when I inhaled the mysterious purple powder I knew a bowel evacuation was coming. That's one way to know it's quality powder, I might add. The quicker the shit, the better the trip is going to be. Lately though, I've been all bound up. So now I'm constipated and paranoid. Unable to deal with the fact that the year was what it was, I destroyed my gel mouse and chucked it at Obermann's head. It all seemed to go by so damn fast.

Obermann caught his breath and said, "Mr. Creel, how you doin', no, no, no, I don't have to take a shit, just...real excited about a fat cat fish I just hooked, gonna throw some water on my face and call him back in fifteen. Let him write the check before I reel him in."

I tried to keep silent, tried to shut down the sounds and smells and nausea that were all rising like a great tropical tide bent on destroying an innocent grass hut village. I could not stop the maddening repetitions that an office worker has to be desensitized to. I could no longer endure the slide of the copying machine accompanied by the brief bright light. The sales pitch went on forever, even on the train ride home, even in the bathroom stall while sitting alone it repeated itself over and over in my head:

"Hello, this is Brian Obermann. I'm just calling to say 'hi' and let you know that your interest in international trade has not been overlooked, and as the largest data warehouse on the planet, The Creel Corporation wants you to know that we are here to support your spirit of business adventure in this exciting global market...."

The salesman's boss replied, "Nice work Brian, reel him in. Say, you got some gooey shit on your neck."

Obermann cooled his face, paper toweled his neck, and thankfully departed from the company's president and the hiding data harvester. Salesmen were ever aware of their own expendability and of the value Creel placed on the tech workers.

Roger Creel chose the stall next to me. A magazine's pages crackled to the ground as the toilet seat slammed down with a force that made me jump.

What an asshole, I thought. Or did I just say that out loud? *He could've cracked the seat—scared the shit outta me. Shit! I haven't shit in days. Toxins are probably spilling out into my system.* Cold sweat had pooled in my armpits and covered my forehead, it crept down my belt line and into the crack of my ass.

Mr. Creel dropped his pants, and the buckle clanged. The magazine opened, I heard a large preparatory inhale, then…gassy discharge, solid waste, plop, and relief. Creel was noisy, stinky, and shameless in his burps, farts, and kerplunking shits.

I dropped my pants and tried to match him. I couldn't crap, though, and the smell and claustrophobia of the metal stall walls were making my head spin. I stood, only to fall back on weak legs.

"Ahhh, mmmm…aahh," Kerplunk! were the sounds of the president dropping another bomb. Fingers that didn't care about preserving it for anyone else turned the crisp magazine's page.

I stood again, opened the door and made it to the sink as Roger Creel wiped his ass. The president was ready to oversee his daily responsibilities, excited by this month's gains in a market that his company monopolized. We sold shipping data to everyone from mafia chop-shop brokerage houses to the UFSA Army. Droplets fell from my face and I began to talk to Creel's reflection without thought or acknowledgement.

"You have a good shit?" I mumbled .

"Excuse me?" he replied, probably wondering why his employee was not using more thought-out speech in order to kiss his now wiped ass like everyone else in the company did.

With a sense of horror, I wondered why I lacked the self-restraint to control my own speech, yet at the same time, I felt exhilarated by saying what was on my mind. I then watched, in initial disbelief, as the demon opened the door on the last stall and walked toward Roger Creel. This three-dimensional waking nightmare was naked, blood red, and appeared to be built to live in fire. His tongue flicked out like a snake's to smell the air as he spoke, "I'm going to stick my fist in Creel's asshole."

I staggered back, almost falling down, compelled by the realism of this hallucination to inform the company's president of the up and coming demonic anal probe. The words spit themselves out, "Mr. Creel, a demon is gonna fist your ass!"

Now it was Creel who stumbled back and, I could have sworn, reached for his asshole, as if to check if it was safe in his pants.

The demon smiled and backpedaled to the last stall, slowly closing the door behind him.

A paralysis overtook me, and a silence so overwhelming that I was sure I had become utterly stone deaf. My first attempt at a step brought me to the cold tile floor, more horrified still that my feet had gotten caught up in the pants and underwear that still remained bunched up around my ankles.

*　　　*　　　*　　　*

I had been escorted out by Security, but not put under arrest. My "In Case Of Emergency" form listed my brother, Alexander, and one of his employees, Nekros, was waiting for me when I got to the lobby.

My previous hospitalization would be taken into account when the Human Services Department reviewed my situation. I would receive a letter indicating that I would be allowed back to work after "further medical examinations," followed by weeks of therapy.

I didn't go back for any of my stuff. I knew I'd never be going back to that office. The evil thing held the door for me on the way out and I kept my eyes forward, hoping it was some temporary illusory effect the damaged computer had left in my eye.

Sixth Avenue's buildings looked like jail cells to me. Random people became so hideous in their desperate walking and *en garde* stances. Young men were all potential assailants, and my heart skipped and my jaw clenched with each bump or stare. My sweating increased, and by the time I got to Nekros's car I was drenched. The demon was sitting in the backseat when the door opened, his hoofed foot dangling from his crossed leg. The vile one took up most of the space. Thankfully, when I slammed the door, Nekros said, "I like the subway better anyway."

Slave To The Grind will help me out, I thought to myself, and when I walked in my escort didn't seem to object. A familiar place, a shelter from the storm of the city's overwhelming sensory stimulation that was raining on me, was becoming an imperative.

I took a corner seat facing the door. Nekros got us coffees. I tried to look at him to say I didn't need Alexander's babysitting, but his face sickened me. Not because it was ugly, but because it was not consistent. One eye grew to be bigger than the other, then shrank and grew again. Puffy cauliflower ears swelled and deflated, hair climbed from his collar and retreated back into his psychedelic shirt; his crooked teeth spun in his mouth like tiny blender blades. Luckily he didn't talk much, just ogled the waitress as she walked by and smiled, rubbing his stubbly black-haired chin.

The coffee was palatable when I closed my eyes, and went down easily in large gulps. I became aware of one thing I hadn't left behind. It pressed against my leg, and once retrieved, I nearly kissed its surface for joy. My journal would save me. The blessed keeper would sift through these mad distractions and expose what was really needing to be released. It was frighteningly clear to me that what I was suffering was not casual, or ordinary, or at all sane. This is the horror, the tiny conscious self that can reflect on a madness that appears overwhelming and indefatigable. I needed something to write with, and before I could finish stuttering out, "p...pp...ppp...pen," Nekros had one in my hand.

*   *   *   *

Swallowing the rest of the hot black liquid I began.

Dear Martha,

Here I am, someone just opened a door behind me, I still write, no footsteps, I wonder if I am welcome. Here I am, after quitting a job I write to celebrate. Quitting, like shitting, has left me pleasantly empty, and indestructible. What will I do? For so long I've wondered. My endurance amazes me. I am here, at a coffee shop, writing, and reading, in celebration of quitting. Just walked out, I am not losing my shit, or going crazy or laughing indiscriminately or zoning out constantly. I am here. This paper and pen and effort combination feels beautifully like a suicide note. A bunch of clean thoughts entering a dirty world, but the cool breeze and invisible birds don't come from my writing. Yes, God gave them to us, to listen to. I can liberate my brothers and sisters, my neighbors, through simplicity. I can learn the stories now that are pregnant with form, archetype, and the truth that makes the citizen stop dead in his tracks, and say no more. I am your whisper dream, the one that slid off the subway, but left footprints in your eyes. The tracks are clear to me, I see your ancient question, and I see your wonder. You're on the breeze now, you will go back yet. You will all return to the connected absurdity that devils reign in, that profit breeds. Darkness has systematically put good thoughts in jail cells, or worse, worse is when a thought is blacklisted from the files of cognition. All good thoughts are mocked by demons of profit. Knowledge, only for power, kindness only for reward. I get sleepy, and tired of this lot, but I never quit. You may hit and hurt but, if it takes all night I will connect, right between your eyes, and you will feel dizzy. "World History is not the arena of happiness, history generates a picture of the most fearful aspect, and stirs emotions of the deepest and most bewildering sadness, counterbalanced by no consolatory result" according to Hegel. No meaning, but to think. The thinker, thinking. No one mentioned knowing or knowledge or reward or challenge to think what has never been thought. NO, just think. What are you doing? Thinking, think about it. I I I and the almighty I. Adventure? Adventure, dime-store novels, wonder if I am afraid to die? Yes, I must be, surely it is the root of unhappiness for me. People kill me by being loan sharks of existence. Loan me a life, and I am indebted to you, ironically this debt is life-denying. Poor boy laughs it up in the woods, with his smile and love of not fearing death, it's close, ain't that the funny part? Separation anxiety, giggle giggle, that is funny. Live free or die, I am an American, identify yourself. Someone just crept up on me, coast is clear, just a friend. Let me tell you about the horrors of being trapped in a weak lifestyle where anger seems absolutely linked to truth. Let me tell you, you gonna let me tell you, you, you, Y.O.U. Superstitious bogey man this is what I am. I am, I am, I am. From quiet marshes, I creep. I bed down with silent things, like alligator and snake, yes snake. Sold, eat my young. Bush men, teach me, here I am, in the woods. Revolution! Again, oh boy, this is gonna be fun, lip smacking tasty, and the best part of all, I don't have to break the law of laws. Love God, love your neighbor, break these, and well, the fight is lost, follow these, and victory! Beguile me a witch, broomstick magic, and veterans of foreign war. All you smiling foreigners who get saved all the time, you've gone and built a giant world, too big to have fun because you don't know anybody. Give me Liberty...who wants to be an American today! Right now, UFSA, UFSA, UFSA. Mommy, daddy, brothers, sisters, uncles, aunts, cousins, grans, cops, cars, critics of all shapes and sizes, are assholes as varied as, other parts, or are they industry standard? Sphincter doors provide the tightest of shields, for doors. Read me a world where we are all aware of wee...wee...I'm on a swing, feet barely touch, going higher and returning, higher and returning. That then which no greater can be thought. That then thar is a thought of gold, light as light, but heavy. The heavy of them all. Interface may change, but the inner face may never, my nose is cold, I *am ready now, to perfume you, sing to you, tuck you in, and teach food gathering, medicine making, shelter building, camouflage, nature's hygiene, here nothing is cosmetic. The real deal, wigwam whammy someone just crept up on me, no knife in her teeth. Whoa, if she read what I write, whoa Nelly, do we need horses. Whoa Nelly, we need Nelly. Strong women make good soup. Invisible people always eat, physically and spiritually, no anger once we're there. Anger is this place's flotation device, we leave anger with profit and money. Freedom through liberation by independence. Independent people do not need governments, only families, friends, holidays, and waves of beautiful, free, and clean thoughts, ride on thought, think yourself away from profit. First step, separation from within. You see, when I'm ready, I'm always welcome. Martha, something is happening that our relationship cannot fix. There is a selfish strangeness in my blood that I will not risk infecting you with.*

Love,

Gus

*   *   *   *

I folded it. Wrote Martha's name and address on the back and slid it over to the morphing man who was sent to watch out for me. I figured as long as he was here, I might as well utilize him. Nekros grinned and looked up at me with one pulsing eyeball. His hairy fingers attached themselves to the letter like tentacles with suction cups.

"*Koreetsi?*" he asked.

The Greek word for girl. He assumed what I wrote was for my girlfriend and smiled a little wider with his rhetorical question, like that fact made my whole breakdown excusable. His grin got wider and his voice came out as if it were air being squeezed from a balloon. "Of course, I bring to her."

I rose. He dropped some coin and followed.

Before we got to the sidewalk I turned to retreat back into the cafe. He moved in front of me and shook out a cigarette. He put one in his own mouth as if I grew up in a jungle where cigarettes didn't exist. The orange tip grew as he inhaled. He gave it to me before lighting another. Everything dies, so everything can live. I smoked and embraced the burn. We walked toward the train.

"You got the letter?" Of course he had it.

"Yeah, I got it." He patted his shirt pocket.

We smoked and I rubbed my hand through my scalp.

Are you aware that by smoking on this sidewalk you are infringing on other people's freedoms? spoke a voice that didn't come from Nekros. Where the hell did that come from now? Not my head…my head wouldn't have said that. I wondered.

"Listen, give a break eh, we have a smoke, then, we go on train." That was Nekros, the ugly Greek guy. He was ugly, actually, for real, like a troll with a ponytail. His Hawaiian shirt didn't help, like a warrior dwarf on vacation in another world.

A metallic dog opened its toothless jaws and toy eyes glowed yellow. A SAM-URAI's companion.

"Are you in possession of a firearm, sir?"

There he was, a Plain Clothes. Well, as plain as they get anyway, the raincoat, the black gloves, and the robotic pet usually gave 'em away. *Did he just ask if Nekros was packing?*

"*Mi estas Speciala Peranto.*" That wasn't Greek, and Nekros said it while aiming his palm at the dog's snout. The dog's nose quivered as if sniffing. Its eyes switched to green.

"*Jes, certe. Mi bedauras.*" The SAM nodded as he spoke, and with robot in tow, walked away.

I held the smoking filter, not sure what to do with it. Nekros squeezed it out with his whole hand and added it to his pocket.

"That place I worked, Nekros, it fucked with me, I had to leave. What happened with the SAM?"

"He fuck with me, I piss on him and his doggy. Fuck the job. Yore brather say you better than that place, anyway."

"He said that?"

Nekros placed his cigarette-butt-smelling palm on one of my scars and gave a firm shake. "Costa…yore brather, he feel real bad, you getting' hurt, hurt because of his bus-i-ness. Don' warry no more, jus' feel better."

People began rising out of the station stairs behind me. His hand was still on my neck and conveyed a man-to-dog affection. A bunch of guys wearing gang-style displays of colors strutted by and one of them coughed and mockingly called us "Fags!" which triggered a cackle of laughter and crotch-grabbing, palm-slapping adolescent agreements.

Nekros's nostrils flared and he spun to face them, and on any other day I bet he would have let them walk, but today I was in bad shape and he was told to take care of me.

"You got something say to me little bitches?"

Oh shit.

"What! What! Stick it to 'em, knock dis fag out yo!"

"Come to me little bitch, I give you something."

Oh shit. Three guys. I can't even swallow. Backing up, going to take off, can't think, gotta run, not another death, not again.

The "little bitch" was actually the biggest one. He responded by looking away from Nekros, as if he conceded to the smaller, troll-like man. I was relieved, until his head turned back toward us, followed by his swinging hand.

Slap! My face, throbbing, stinging instantly, nostril trickling blood, lip quivering, eyes watering.

"Yo bitch ass friend's scared you ugly fuck, he gonna piss his pants!"

More laughs, gold teeth, I see knuckles and clenched fists, new-looking boots, sinewy muscles, anger, rage, the deadly age of brash decisions and giant pride. Tada, the subway, hospitals and doctors, cops, loss. *Where's a SAMURAI when you need one?*

The back of Nekros's hand shoved me. What was he going to do against three fired-up thugs? Wait, the dog's eyes, the SAM asking if he had a gun. What is Alex into if this guy works for him? Not this, not now.

"Who will be ugly today?"

"What?" their Alpha shouted.

I was puzzled too, but that was their mistake, to be puzzled instead of ready. The loudest one was confused, and got in his face before Nekros began to go to work.

I wanted it to happen, willed it to happen, wished it was me doin' it at that moment. But I just stood there, half of me scared, half of me hating. I didn't see the demon though, and this was all very real.

Nekros pressed the pistol against the loud one's gut, the muzzle disappearing. One of them almost ran until Nekros commanded him to "Stay!"

They all looked at me like I was our gang's ringleader or something—some kind of kingpin my monkey-faced crony was defending.

Nekros knew what he was doing. And expertly controlled the situation as he walked the whole group down the side street and into a restaurant's alley.

"Come Gus, it okay, dis is bus-i-ness."

I followed, excited that I wasn't being beaten, took it to another level and pushed one of them, the one who gave me the hardest look, the one who had slapped me. I told him he could walk away, I gave him the chance that Tada didn't give me. He stupidly pushed back and Nekros hit him hard with the butt of the gun. He went down and I watched his hands try to climb my legs. Nekros restored the pistol to the holster on his lower back hidden beneath his shirt, then, like the heat that dropped from ancient catapults, unleashed Greek fire.

He used his head to batter faces, grabbed crotches and squeezed like crushing grapes, applied knee to chin, tore out an ear ring, twisted fingers until they popped, elbowed down onto vertebrae, and picked one up to execute a suplex-style throw. The punks were moaning and crawling and Nekros kept kicking and stomping and raging. The broken leader, his ear lobe hanging like a fish on a hook, retrieved a small plastic bag of restaurant garbage, probably containing nothing more than old salad and rotten eggs, and came for Nekros's back. My stillness, like a SAMURAI on a subway, must have made me invisible because he didn't see me when I hit him. I had never hit anyone before, and when my fist snapped against his lip it made it pop like a ketchup packet. I walked right in front of him, looked him in his face as he swung at my comrade, and struck him in his offending mouth.

The mad Greek turned just as I did it. Perhaps my violence gave him a feeling of completion. He grabbed my wrist and we briskly walked out of the alley and found ourselves in a crowd. We disappeared and reemerged only to steal down another side street.

Nekros sat down, panting, and waggled his hand for me to join him. People walked by, the streets became busier. We just blended in. He lit a cigarette and placed the pack and lighter between us.

I didn't wait for him to offer me one. I lit up. The red on my knuckle didn't transform into anything and didn't feel like a metaphor, yet I was now in possession of a knowledge I never had. Not in this life anyway. I asked for the letter back. Nekros cupped the back of my neck and smiled. His brutal face was ancient and loyal. I felt less alone and a part of some mad old clannish world. The actual business of things did not go on display in our civilized System. Reality was blood; often silent, ever present, always red.

CHAPTER 7

▼

HALL OF ILLUSION

Joker you are...
alone
little man of
lost lessons of
head examining sessions
a questing beast
awed by apocalyptic processions
word digester
knowledge protester
feelings fester
reason pesters
Act 2
young
Court Jester.

There is a man who ate too much LSD in the 1970s and began to see a monstrous blob, which caused him to run, hide, and call the police for help. His trip ended, the nightmare remained. No pill, nor hospital, nor words could stop the blob's relentless chase, and the man was going mad. One day he entered a pool hall and his nightmare stopped. The crack of balls and squeak of chalk kept the creature at bay for reasons unknown to the medical world. If he still lives today, this man is the fly on the wall in some smoky room full of felt-covered tables. If you shoot stick, look around for the guy who really loves being there and has no desire to leave. There might be a hideous monster outside waiting for him.

*　　*　　*　　*

The little therapy I had entertained was somewhat interesting, and I hoped that the act of going would have eased Alexander's guilt. I learned a few things, but it didn't help me when the demon approached. When I found out that Roger Creel, great-great grandson of the original pirate who first profited from selling cargo information was hospitalized for cancer of the colon, my dark daydreams became even more mockingly real.

I like psychology, but not therapy; I enjoy analysis, but not being analyzed. When the doctor suggested that a psychoactive drug would help me cope with my delusions, I walked out. Just like that. Master of my own fate. Captain of my own soul. Will to power, slave to no one. It was all up to me.

Some days I was too scared to leave the apartment. Other days my own room spat me out to search for sanity. I slept only if I got tired enough to pass out. I didn't work and was embarrassed that Alex was paying my rent.

Things weren't good between Martha and me. It wasn't fair. Sometimes I wished she would just dump me, and wondered if she was sticking it out for some stupid guilty reason.

One day I ran practically the entire length of Manhattan Island. It started out as a pleasant walk. I was looking for William again. I just wanted to talk with him, maybe hear a story. I opened the Harlem café's door, heard the jazz and smelled the wonderful bread. The heat from the kitchen was inviting and the iron stove let out steam as the door fell open. But when the steam cleared it was the horned head of the monster that came out.

His stringy red torso unfolded like a Hindu god emerging from a magic box. The hands came down first with vein-filled arms and black claws for his fingernails. When the little boy, Santo, ran by the repulsive eyes followed him. With a perverse smile it exposed its backside that had adopted the form of a giant serpent. The tongue flicked out at the blind patrons. Swimming the café's floor it moved beneath tables and in between legs.

I had to leave because I couldn't stand feeling so powerless. I knew he would always be working his dark tricks. Every minute of the day; injecting cancers, whispering lies, goading jealousies, feeding vanities and egos and insecurities. I wasn't good enough to stop him. I could only see him, and it wasn't a gift, it was a curse. Running away made my legs hurt and my lungs tear open and put my focus in my gut. My temples pounded with blood and when I finally stopped, I vomited.

I heard someone say I was a "damn junky." Leaning against a signpost I started to laugh out loud and felt almost as mad as I must've appeared. They looked like tourists weekending in the Village. What they couldn't see was the devil at their feet, small but growing, getting taller with each angry word.

*　　　*　　　*　　　*

On Sunday I sat with Martha on a bench in Astoria Park. The waters beneath the Hell's Gate Bridge crashed against rocks, their turbulence mirroring my thoughts. The card I flipped in my fingers gave me intermittent calm as the waters of my mind foamed and swirled, seeking new path.

The address Nekros gave me was way uptown in the Bronx. Martha was against me going. I hadn't told her what had happened in the alley, she still didn't like Nekros. Said he gave her a bad feeling. Nekros referred to the place simply as The Gym.

*　　　*　　　*　　　*

It was 5:30 when we arrived, and a summery breeze foreshadowed a cool evening. A Moslem man rolled up a prayer rug and brought it into the bodega he worked in. The Gym appeared like a dark castle, sitting ominously on a rough block and seemingly demanding a mysterious respect. Its door opened slowly, as cast iron usually does. The air was heavy with exertion.

Deception was the first thing I thought. No one could tell from the outside, or even from the concrete foyer, just how enormous this room actually was. Where did it all come from, and how could it stay so hidden? Weight plates clanked, jump ropes whirled, and leather met leather as fists and feet and shins and elbows hammered punching bags. No machines to help you get more reps, and no TVs to dissolve your pain when hitting a new endurance goal on a treadmill. No personal trainers with collared shirts and white towels to motivate the shrinking of your fat ass. No smoothies or masseuses here. Just sweat and skill, and the ancient laws of combat.

Two barefoot guys were going toe to toe in the ring. They wore fingerless padded gloves and shin guards. The strikes were fast, and before the door behind me shut, one of them was on the ground with his arm getting hyper-extended. *This place is for real*, I thought and squeezed Martha's hand to let her know that I had a good feeling.

Since there wasn't a front desk to inquire at, I just walked on in. Everyone was busy and absorbed in what they were doing. Nekros was in the ring examining the downed fighter's elbow, bending the arm two or three times before giving him a clean bill of health with a, "You are fine, next time tap out faster. Go shower."

He saw us. "Yasou, Gus! I be right there!" Sliding through the ropes he walked over and hugged me.

He took Martha's hand and shook it as gently as meat hooks could do. "Very nice to meet you, you the lovely Martha, I presume."

His accent did make him sound kind of slimy, and I knew Martha thought even worse of him. Like she was struggling to say it, "Hello, Ne...kros. This place is...huge."

Silence. Perhaps that translated strangely.

"Yeah," I interjected, "You got quite a gym here."

"Thanks to Aleco, yore brather. Come, I show you aroun'."

Martha and I exchanged puzzled glances when our host wasn't looking. On the tour our first stop was an in-progress silat class. Sweating students sat cross-legged against a matted wall, eyes fixated on every move being made before them. The instructor held a silver practice blade and danced in and out of range as a thick hairy man wearing a snow-white padded shirt swung a club in her direction.

A butterfly fluttering. Each time she slashed a red line appeared on the attacker. Parry, dance, slash, 1, 2, 3. Parry, dance, slash, 1, 2, 3. It was beautiful. The power of the man's body had no effect. Each time he encroached she yielded slightly, then the blade slashed from what would seem an awkward position. By the time she stopped he was a large, perspiring candy cane.

The slasher, who wore a sweatshirt with a worn out NYPD logo in the upper corner, switched the fake knife to her left hand before introducing herself. Her speech had a Latin twang to it, and despite her long black hair and curvaceous body that couldn't be hidden by baggy sweat clothes, she was macho. Her histrionics were intimidating and her voice scratchy as if she had fought off choke holds many times.

"What up, Greek? Who you got for me now? Mr. and Mrs. Diplomat scared to be livin' in New Yowk?"

Martha's hand got hot, and both our faces reddened.

Nekros introduced us. "Candy, this is Mr. Cast's brother Gus, and his friend,...ehhh...Marr-tha."

Candy jammed the knife in the waistband of her sweatpants and covered up her sarcasm with quick slapping handshakes and half-hugs, her weapon pressing against my hip when she embraced me. I tried to stare at her practice partner's mock wounds to distract myself from the semi-awkward situation.

"Ohh, why didn't you tell me, Greek? Well, welcome to The Gym—training ground for security professionals, stomping ground for Special Agents!"

Candy rolled one shoulder toward me and before I knew what was going on she was holding my open palm up for everyone to see and pulling the practice blade across it. "Red handed!" She broke into laughter as she decorated her own palm to show Martha. "See, it's just ink, honey."

"Okay, Candy, get back to work," Nekros smilingly prompted, as if she had said too much, too soon.

As we walked to the free-weight area to meet Serge, a former UFR Special Forces soldier, Candy shouted, "We'll play some pool later, grab a beer upstairs!"

"Sounds good!" Martha and I replied in stereo. I tried to rub out the ink and Martha stuck a cleaning towelette in my hand. Following a thick, dark brown banister that had lost its shine many years ago, we climbed cold, black stone stairs into silence, the sound of workouts fading with each step. We came to a cloudy glass door that had been painted with the words,

PANKRATION SOCIETY SOCIAL CLUB.

A black-and-white tiled floor, supporting round wooden tables with red vase centerpieces, was as surprising as the large workout room. Hanging green glass fixtures cast a soothing light. A crooner's music played in the background, Tony Bennett I guessed. "Old-fashioned and original" is what the jukebox and pool tables and general ambience conveyed to me. A small stage hosted a lonely microphone, and a bar was stocked with legions of colorful bottles, its brick-red leather stools inviting.

Nekros explained over cold green bottles that pankration was the ancient Greek combat sport that combined all fighting styles. Alexander chose the name because he hoped The Gym would be the melting pot for training his security people in all the world's martial arts, and that the club would be where the most effective ideas could rise to the top. All the instructors were Special Agents as recognized by the UN's Secular Army. Remarkable, I thought. But contract security was a huge business, and that is what Alex did best—business.

Nekros apologized for serving beer, but said that they had no bartender to mix drinks. We clanked bottles before he took us to the basement, where a soundproof pistol range topped the day's surprises. Martha made a joke about meeting James Bond's hapless scientist, Q.

"Most of dis building was old factory. City was going to destroy before Aleco saved it."

"Most?" I asked.

Sounding now like he had said too much, "Ahh, yeah, da top floor, it was a karate school or somethin'. Funny, hah?"

∗   ∗   ∗   ∗

Serge drove us home, despite our weak protests. We fiddled with the backseat radio and stared through tinted windows at the whizzing lights The trip back to Queens took a long time, and fatigue put us both into a weird daze.

As I said goodbye to Serge before closing the car's door, he asked me, "What time?"

"Excuse me?"

"What time I pick you up? You will train…yes?"

"Ahhh…yes, I'll be there, thanks, I'll get there on my own."

"Yahhh, sure, tomoorow."

"See you tomorrow."

Martha was already keying in the door when she asked, "What was that all about?"

"I said I might see him again, if I want to workout there." Deception—it's a terribly tricky thing.

∗   ∗   ∗   ∗

Martha was running late the next morning. She didn't have time to do her usual hot-yoga before showering. I know she was tired, too, because Wyeth had come home close to midnight, and at two o'clock had to be asked to lower the TV. He usually went into the shop after lunch on Sundays and worked till 8 or 9, often finishing the day at a pub, and always leaving a very used water bong in an unlikely and unseen place.

Martha's foot found his hiding spot. The stinky filter water splashed her stockings "You shit!" she screamed, acknowledging his unlearned lesson.

He wouldn't budge, I knew that; he slept corpselike, and to try and arouse him one often had to bear witness to his fat, ultra-white stark naked form. I could've gotten up though, got her a change of clothes, or at least made an attempt to clean the spill. But no, instead I lay in bed staring at my clock, compounding her suffering by fake sleeping. What a shit.

* * * *

I had breakfast with Wye at around 11. It was like old times, and he even asked me if I wanted him to call in sick. I explained my plan, sharing with him my deceit and convincing myself I could follow through with it at the same time. The N train to the D, no problem.

"You know that switch is where…well, you know." He was referring to the place in the subway terminal where Yoshitsuru Tada tried to murder me.

"Yeah, Wye, I know where it is."

"And you're okay with that?"

I gave him a burning look that would make anybody who wasn't my best friend think that I wanted to do him grave harm. But this way that I peered deep into Neederman's bloodshot eyes told him what words could not.

"Yeah, you know what you're doing."

"Thanks Wye…pass the soy milk please."

* * * *

Martha didn't like Nekros, she didn't want me hanging around a world that subsisted on violence, and she didn't enjoy the thought of me rubbing up against hot knife-wielding women. Most of all, she didn't want me to break down; not without her there to help, not at night, and not in the subways.

Yesterday, the train switch was quiet. It was Sunday, and I could talk with Martha about what she wanted to do about graduate school, or laugh at her people-watching jokes, or just squeeze her hand when I thought I saw something coming that probably wasn't there at all.

This Monday the crowds were moving like bleeding cattle that had been punctured by the arrows of Diana the Huntress. This day was for venerating the moon, not for commuting. They all pay for this offence with lances of misery, and pray for the day of beauty to come and the replacement of the angry archer. These people were walking in the daydream of the week's end coming, and awaiting the spiral light of Venus on Friday night. Waiting for the moment when they could all look up drunkenly and apologize to the grand scheme they had offended.

So I didn't mind when they bumped into me, cut me off, or took my seat. They were stuck in the trenches, while I was just a ghost. A former one of them, no longer productive, useless and nearly invisible.

Off the N train and onto the platform I waited for the Express. It had to be quick tonight, that's for sure, all these people needing to feed their kids and pay their bills and bring home silly trinket gifts for their girlfriends. Not me, I was going to The Gym. I tried not to make eye contact with anyone in the terminal, and was wishing I had brought sunglasses. I remembered my I.D. and memory and phone cards. I even had a small bottle of oxygenated water and vitamin-C lozenges. If I had dark glasses, even if I was looking at someone, they wouldn't be able to tell. Like the guy leaning against the tiled wall, he might've been looking at me, but then again, maybe not. I couldn't stop thinking about it once my focus locked. I put three orange tabs in my mouth.

I wished that train would arrive. This guy, he wasn't like everybody else, and he might've been staring at me. If I could move like Candy, I wouldn't have been sweating like I was. If I could unleash my inner gladiator like Nekros, this situation wouldn't have bothered me. If I could disappear and reappear somewhere else like a comic book super hero then, well, I guess I wouldn'ta done what I did.

I approached him, not from the side, but head on. Looked right into his face, it worked before, and gave him the opportunity to show me who he was. He didn't budge. I wondered if he could hear me, then I thought it was a trick, then got scared because I might've just been speaking in my head and not to him. He was still. Straight shiny black hair, light brown skin, a blue letterman's jacket and baggy pants. Headphones, old-fashioned ones, hugged his ears. Of course, he couldn't hear me because he wore big old muffling headphones just like the ones Tada wore.

Tada! No. Why won't he take them off, then? The stare, I'll give him the stare and won't have to talk. I'll pierce right through the cheap plastic mirrors and tell him that…that…he has fiery patterns swirling in two small storms, that he is possessed of darkness and servant to the devil!

His hands were moving inside his jacket pockets. I wasn't running. He flinched, as if he would have taken a step back if the wall wasn't there. His hands were creeping out, coming together, raising something to show me. A heart! A black, pulsing, evil heart! The tip of a long red tail smacked the floor, falling hard out of his pants.

I ran. It's what worked. But I was in a crowded terminal. I hid behind a garbage can, then ran some more. When I got up my head was light. Must have stood too fast. I collided with a newspaper stand. Knocked some stuff over. The guy screamed, a lady with a powerful piercing voice followed. The sounds were terrifying, did they see the abomination coming? The sounds stopped abruptly, save for the shuffle of the mob's feet.

The SAMURAI turned me around and hugged me against an armored chest. A foot tapped just above my calf and I was on my knees. The floor looked so cold when empty.

"Atendu! Atendu!"

The voice made the SAMURAI take notice and step in front of my kneeling form. My wrists were bound. Where the hell was the...? There was no demon, was there? The black heart? A gel mouse. Portable, probably illegal. The glasses, virtual screens.

Another hallucination. I wanted to scream and let this cop know there was no cruel evil being chasing me. That I had made a mistake, had imagined it all, and that everything was fine. I would have liked to say these things, but something the SAM had done had rendered me speechless. It was going to be okay, though, because this new voice was saying it all for me, and in the language the cop listened to.

"Mi estas Speciala Peranto. Li estas PANKRATION-ano."

Serge was picking me up after all, and apparently pleading my case.

"Ne gravas," the arresting SAM replied.

Serge extended his arm, kneeled, and allowed the mechanical dog to sniff his palm.

My rescuer continued, now looking up at the SAM as if he were his confessor. *"Bonvolu auskulti pli atenteme, mi petas. Mi estas Speciala Peranto."*

He was sounding desperate, I had no idea what he was saying.

The SAM looked down at his robot. A beautiful shade of holiday green began to glow, like two little ornaments.

Merry Christmas! Get me outta these cuffs.

✳   ✳   ✳   ✳

The SAMURAI walked us out of the eerily quiet section of terminal. The silent alarms that affected the nervous system and directed crowds to disperse were being turned off as the bright-eyed mutt strutted by. Like ocean water filling in a sand castle's moat, the people fell in behind us.

Serge's black car was waiting. The large bearded man who was diced and sliced in practice was in the passenger seat.

"Hi ya doin', Gus?"

Whaddya know, a regular tri-state American working for Alex. I wanted to reply coolly with the same question, but found myself unable to speak

"It's all right kid, ma bad, the fuckin'...beams that shoot out, ya know, the silent alarms, they'll shut ya up for a while."

I nodded toward Serge as if to say, *Bullshit, Sasquatch, the Russian robot over here was making small talk with the SAM.*

Apparently he read my nod well. "Oh, very perceptive, Serge is all chipped up. One in the ear, one in the palm. Special Agent privileges."

So that's how they did it. The Golden Rule: the one with the gold rules. Forget the Secular Army socialism, the feed-the-world, safety-first crap. You got the bancos, they got the implants. Reality is red. Damn. I shouldn'ta hit that kid.

*   *   *   *

My tongue loosened when we rolled up to The Gym. We parked behind Alexander's electric Porsche. Several vehicles gave off an out-of-place shine on this inner city street, like healthy, ripe fruit growing in the winter's snow.

When we entered, Big Bobby (Big Bobby with the beard) asked me if I was thirsty or hungry. I shook my head to say no. "Are ya sure? I can make ya a sandweech."

"No." It came out with respectful intention, but sounded rude. "No thanks, Bobby."

He smiled and led the way down stairs. Serge followed, almost disappearing in silence and mechanical behavior. Serge had a blank affect, no emotion in his words, nothing wasted in his movement. Maybe he saved it all up for talking to SAMURAI cops about letting delusional people go.

The bare cinder-block basement stairs led to a clear sliding door. Before pushing on the bulletproof plastic, we all put soft orange things in our ears. As it slid open, *pop pop...pop, pop pop...pop* sounds echoed. The range was open and empty. No lanes with targets that slide back and forth like in the FBI movies. There were barriers, and pop-ups, and columns to run behind. The corners of the room were deep black shadows. Alexander was making the noise.

He wore one gun under his arm and one on his belt. *Pop pop...pop.* He fired as he took a knee. When the target fell, Alex continued to aim the weapon and ran toward a stacked-brick wall. Reholstering that firearm, he retrieved the second.

We sat behind a table and behind more thick plastic as if we were about to judge an event. Alexander was wearing a tailored suit, like he just got in from a meeting and had no time to change. Hard knee pads matched his attire in blackness. Amber-glossed glasses seemed to separate him from everything but the act of shooting.

"Lights!" he yelled, sounding like an impassioned director.

Bobby flicked a switch. We all disappeared. A spring boinged, then a silver shine,

Pop pop...pop!. Boing! Shine. Pop pop...pop!

This happened three more times. In the dark things moved and I tried closing my eyes. It was here, in this crazy hidden world. Hiding in one of those corners, free now in the darkness. Alex? It would get to Alex, he was in the way.

"Alex! Shoot it! Shoot it! It's right behind you!"

What the fuck was I talking about, my God am I a real live crazy person? Should I be taking the anti-psychotic drugs? These are Alex's friends, his workers, his place, what am I doing? Crying, that's what; I started to cry. *Gotta run, gotta go!* My feet made a scuffle.

"Grab him! Keep him here!" It was Alexander yelling now, commanding his people to stop me. Then giving the stage directions again, "Lights! Put the fucking lights on Bobby!"

Klick.

Pupils shrinking. Serge and Bobby, giant book ends. But Alex, holy shit, I can't go on like this. I don't even believe what I'm seeing now. Not the hoofed prince of darkness anymore, that fear can be more easily understood, archetypes and bad Sunday school teachers. This time, this fear, was more real. I was seeing Tada, the Asian kid who came for me and didn't do his job right. The son of a bitch who made me into this crying sack of pathetic sickness.

"Bring him here guys." His voice was toned down. "Gus, Gus...." He was teary. The grips on my arms let up, just supporting my weight, guiding my direction. He dropped the shooting glasses to the floor and returned the piece to his belt.

"Gus, come on over, there is nothing here that's gonna hurt you." He reached back and touched Tada's face. In a sense it was real, a hologram cast over a target dummy. The colors that made up his face danced as Alex clawed into the image's head.

"It's a picture, Gus; a picture of the motherfucker who jumped you but couldn't stop you." He drew his larger, shoulder-holstered weapon and jammed it hard into the cheek of the dummy.

"I am sorry you ever got involved, Gus. This piece of shit broke the code, but now he's gone." The barrel pushed deeper, and his voice got grittier. "There's no coming back. Now walk over here, and take this gun, and put a bullet in this piece of shit."

Bobby got behind me and helped me to cradle the pistol in both my hands. Positioning me about five feet from Tada's head, all my focus funneled down the barrel. It was *him*, and this moment was beyond surreal. Time faded and I went back to the crime, staring into the attacker's face, the subway wall behind him. Farther back—my life, it can't be accidental, everything has meaning. Tada's life, our souls. Meeting like this, briefly, murderously. He was ready. It is all for a reason?

"Do it Gus! Shoot this prick."

So I did.

Bamm!

Louder than a pop, explosive, right between the eyes.

The projector clicked off, the canvas-skinned dummy stood mute, torn and powder burned.

Tada was gone, for good.

CHAPTER 8

▼

DETACHMENT

Rumble
dusk
sun in clouds stretched with a spackle knife.
An eye in the sky
ominous
beautiful
only thing beautiful
cars and people roll under the setting sun,
I judge the world
and am hurt.
The canvas of the sky
is the strangest shade of blue
pink, orange, and the white of clouds.
I have become
parched
empty
under the setting sun
do I give away my life force
with honesty?
Dead in a car
an unpublished poet's notebook
was found miraculously
and his words have scorched

the masses
leather notebooks are now all the rage.
A sky writer unzipped the picture
slowly, memorably
a long, thin, artificial
cloud
all my teachers
have faith
all my hate
cooled by prayer
leaves instructions sizzled into my world
and I am the most fortunate person
because, although I have choice
I do not
in how I see sky, and skin
and answer questions with my pen…
Some words must never be read
the park is closing
will they lock me in?
A collection will be ready for Christmas,
gifts for my friends, closure, and
a will, and epitaph
to mark decisions
accept me or leave me
the canvas is more gray
a dog coughs up a bushel of hay
and leaves it in the road
for a poet to dodge
and trigger the flip
and Hollywood explosion.
The detective who finds the leather notebook
has a poetic side
but doesn't much care for doing art
he read it though
when he was drunk
in his office with a bottle
he likes this kid
and wants to get the notebook

to the family
but the drive to the dead poet's house is long
too much time to think
about the words
he gives the parents a ten-dollar pen instead
says it was in the car
the notebook is sitting
underneath the nearly empty bottle.
The sky
looks stranger
every day.

I finally caught up with William. A year had passed since our last meeting. The scarf he wore gave him the appearance of a British fighter pilot just in from a dogfight with the Red Baron. The café was so packed with eccentrics that day that William and I just blended in. This was his specialty after all, blending in, becoming invisible. A secret I still wished to learn.

Running next door after putting in our order, I bought the most expensive pack of cigarettes I could find and just placed them on our table. William gave a polite nod before taking one. I nodded back and lit it for him. It feels good to give respect where it is due. Settling in, letting the jazz do its work, I pictured pearls of wisdom pooling in his pockets and waited for the gift of just one.

"My dear boy, how's your sex life?"

Things had changed. The Gym had become my identity. I was twenty pounds of muscle heavier, had hard, calloused fists, tied my hair back in a ponytail, and was having sexual relations with several exotic dancers who frequently worked at the social club.

"Well, Martha and I are really just friends now."

He looked remorseful, but not surprised.

I fumbled out a cigarette even though my training forbade it. William smiled knowingly and lit it.

We discussed the psychiatrist's diagnosis. According to her, the dark visions I experienced were the energy I gave to the emptiness of my trauma. Because my attacker killed himself and never had to answer for his crimes, I could not have closure. The attack would continue in various, often bizarre forms until I saw its end psychologically. Alexander had secretly planned my trauma's finale with the good doctor, and, like some reworked Hitchcock plot, ended my neurosis.

I jabbered on for quite a while, intellectually at times. I told him of the martial arts I had been learning, and of the women I entertained, and how I was the club's bartender and of all the strange and good books I had been finding and reading. No one else I knew would understand. I asked him, at last, if he would teach me about disappearing and reappearing.

His great hand smoothed over his own bare scalp and I swore I could hear it like sandpaper scraping. His crystal-ball head being rubbed by his large, homeless hand drowned out all the other sounds, the many conversations and doors bouncing closed and wonderful music. His fingers made circles as he inhaled on the smoking stick; like someone rubbing his belly and chewing gum at the same time, it seemed absurdly comical, but I was now caught in this single peculiar picture and the room faded away along with sounds and smells.

A white cloud bellowed forth, then two streams of dragon smoke; then, as the music and voices and good smells and everyday clings and clangs and coffee mugs being set down on tables returned, William, once in plain view, had vanished.

I was going to play it cool. Then the self-doubt crept in. He wasn't here, but was he ever? Could I have been conversing this whole time with an empty chair? I placed the cigarette in my lips but nothing happened. It had gone out. I crossed my legs, keeping the butt in my mouth, and patted myself down for a lighter. A flame appeared, and I inhaled and followed the fire with my eyes to an arm that led to William Ringle, mysterious master of invisibility. I breathed out in relief and let my puzzled look do all the questioning.

"A thankful spirit creates no friction; having neither equal nor opposite reaction, there is nothing to perceive."

He prayed. That was his secret. Giving thanks can alter the very state of one's existence. The rest of the day was unlike any day that had come before it. I was appreciative, and the more thankful I was, I realized the more there was to be thankful for. A litany wrote itself, much as sediment piles up to form a mountain.

I walked fearlessly for the first time. I knew how William did it. It was the common knowledge of children, vaulted up but always waiting to save us from ourselves.

*   *   *   *

The PANKRATION Society Social Club hosted members and guests of members. I kept it clean, restocked toilet paper, and mixed drinks for tips. I watched many whispery meetings take place in between card games and pool.

The music was never too loud, and strippers or other rented entertainment had to be out before I locked the doors for the night.

This evening I poured sake for two Japanese men. They were SAMURAI, new in this city, and being shown around by Big Bobby. Both men kept it formal, and when Candy approached, did slight bows without getting up from their stools. Her hair was wet and draped over both their shoulders as she pried herself in between them. Candy hugged their waists and stretched forward, letting her large breasts push through a damp T-shirt, invading their "face" space and chipping their hard veneer. As the blushing cops lowered their heads, Candy and I exchanged smiles and had to smile at the elite policemen's awkward humility.

"How 'bout a beer, babe?" she requested cheerfully.

I popped a top and cleared a space between the two officers' porcelain cups. Sato-san and Captain Morehei glanced up from their wine and raised smiling eyebrows at each other. I introduced them to Candy, and then to the knife-throwing target, which kept them thoroughly satisfied until Bobby showed up. That's the type of stuff Alexander's guys appreciated, and the extra effort made me feel more like I was really earning my keep.

I slept upstairs. What Nekros had told me was an old karate school was actually the remnants of the Yama-Arashi Jujutsu Dojo. It had not been touched since the '90s when the school's founder passed away. The space I moved into was the Sensei's former bedroom. It was tiny, I imagine as small as the post-war Tokyo hotel room he had rented at the turn of the last century. I was learning about the man from what he left behind, and from Candy's stories.

My quarters had a straw mat to sleep on, a traditional head pillow, an old (still functioning) electric hot plate, and a meditation table, which I stocked with incense. Sometimes I shared the space with a street cat I named Muso. My new arrangement often found me alone flipping through the faded books that covered the walls and were stacked in piles in the corners. Neatly written letters and diaries and black-and-white photos attached me to a deeper sense of history, which I selfishly hoarded. Like a snobby museum curator or librarian studying ancient treasures after hours, I perused fragile pages with clean hands and under dim light.

A *wakizashi*, picked up on an island battlefield, marked the wall space above where Basil's wrinkled postcard stayed tacked. The sword's scabbard was decorated in places by bits of sea-blue wood. Its original owner must not have been a large man, nor was he an officer. However, the weapon had been unsheathed many times before its carrier met his end in the sights of Sensei Pasito's M-1 rifle.

I trained in the daytime with kickboxing, grappling, knife work and bludgeons. I learned to defend others and myself against multiple attackers. I pumped weights and attacked punching bags and lost myself in the single-minded focus of the martial arts. I cleaned the school and padlocked doors when everyone else went home. Some afternoons I borrowed a car and tried to make it to a park just outside the city before the sun finished setting.

Late at night, I often meditated in the large canvas-matted upstairs dojo. With my back to the wall, I sat beneath two portraits. One photo was of Sensei Pasito, standing proud and gripping the sheathed sword. The other was a mysterious sketch. The individual's face that hung next to Pasito's was partially hidden by cascading straight hair. Although it lacked the resolution of a photo, it was clearly of an older male of Asian ancestry.

With car lights often running shadowy images on the wood-paneled walls, I concentrated on my breathing and the lessons I learned from William. I found timelessness often, and on more than one occasion was aroused by morning sunlight from some deep other world.

One night while the litany of invisibility recited itself in my head, I watched Muso softly leap to the sill. The cat turned its head and used its eyes to experience the world. Muso scanned the darkness with glowing orbs and gazed upon an empty room.

I opened my own eyes wide and observed Muso in the miracle of motion. As the feline stepped I unwrapped myself from the lotus. She stalked a shadow made from a blinking streetlight, I stalked Muso. The cat's name came from feudal Japan, and was borne by the man who had defeated the legendary Musashi.

Miyamoto Musashi, The Sword Saint, met with a man called Muso after more than sixty of his own victorious duels. In a forest, in the solitude of nature, this old fellow who wielded only a blunt cane defeated the world's greatest swordsman. Brought down by Muso's hanbo, Musashi's life was spared and changed forever.

Serge tutored me in the Way of the Stick. His reverence for this simple hanbo weapon and the story behind it guided my training and strengthened my discipline.

The cat Muso pounced on the shadow and I froze. "In the end, you simply must believe," is what William had taught me about becoming invisible. When the cat paused again, I reached out slowly with one finger and gently made contact with her orange fur. Muso leaped!

I smiled in the knowledge of my new gift.

*　　　*　　　*　　　*

Sometimes Candy would join me in the Sensei's old room. She was softer without her clothes on and would open up like a spring rose coming to life when we made love. Incense burned, and we touched each other in an almost ceremonial way to start our night. Thumbing through books and talking in low voices to each other about ancient peoples who had lived simple, healthy lives followed dreamy pillow sessions.

Candy never stayed until morning because of her strong superstition regarding the Sensei. Wearing my old bathrobe and sipping a raspberry tea, Candy told me about Pasito's darker side. You see, she had known him when she was a neighborhood child. Her family lived around the block, and he was her first instructor.

Candita looked over her shoulder and got close to my ear before telling me, "Some used to say he studied the black arts and was obsessed with immortality as he got older. I know he had *mago*, and I always got chills when I was alone with him. His smile, it was so…devilish."

"Hmmm…" was all I could mutter back, keeping my eyes on the pages of the *Nei Ching*, the oldest book of medicine.

Candy put her cup down and knelt, resting her hands on her thighs and letting the soft cotton garment fall open. "I think he still hangs around here, walking the halls like an old *bruja*," she said, holding a far off gaze.

I admired the beauty of the sword's scabbard that seemed to float before my sight. Its sea-colored pattern reminded me of water. I dreamed of the ocean with waves rising in accordance with the moon's glow.

*　　　*　　　*　　　*

It was nearly the end of April, and Alexander made sure I knew that Easter was coming. He told me this via videophone. He was always traveling the United Free Lands, facilitating agreements, promoting emerging technologies, arranging security accounts and conducting business. He was an emerging-technologies executive in at least three corporations, and an influential investor in more companies than I knew. His long arm of influence seemed to have no end. It shouldn't have surprised me that he had arranged a 3-D visit from Demetrios on Easter Sunday. Our youngest brother would appear by hologram, beamed all the way from a mountain base in Eastern Europe. It was ironic—he was fighting in the Balkans, the same lands whose violence had sent our grandfather to America generations before.

I had become good at ignoring ideas that might paralyze my thinking. I didn't think about the danger Demetri was always in, or the horrible ignorance of war. I let the violence of Alexander's world become normal; in fact, I embraced it. Whenever a crooked cop hung out at the club, I served him a drink and pretended all cops were crooked. When payoffs and deals and all manner of illegal business were conducted on the tables that I cleaned, I told myself it was all just that—business—and the business of the world was not something to be questioned.

*　　*　　*　　*

Eastern Orthodox Easter was the last Sunday of the month, and was traditionally celebrated at midnight on Saturday, with the Resurrection Service and the subsequent Liturgy often lasting past two AM. I would take the bus into Nineamoth, New Jersey. I had no desire to show up in church with Nekros. He offered a ride, but I knew he was only going out of loyalty to Alex. I learned early on that Nekros was not the church-going type.

In recent observations while traveling unseen, I had come to realize that there were many invisible people. Most of them did it unconsciously, and carried with them a sadness that emanated from deep within their core. These people could not see themselves, and had become ghosts among the living.

In the shadow of an exiting passenger I stepped from the bus and looked at the luxury cars that packed the roadsides. It was nearly nine PM, and I was back in a town that seemed to be comprised of wall-to-wall suburban mansions. Twice-a-year churchgoers parallel-parked across from police street flares. The wealthiest Greeks in New Jersey attended, dressed to the hilt for this special night.

I wore a dark suit, compliments of Alex. He had Nekros pick it up for me from the same place I would imagine he got all the bodyguards' threads. It wasn't uncomfortable, but didn't fit well either. With the slightly baggy garment on, along with my long hair and scraggly face, you'd think I was straight from Eastern Europe. All I needed was a cigarette and Nekros's accent to complete the disguise.

I moved through the crowd outside the church unnoticed. Small children wearing hard, painful shoes skipped and tripped into women's big butts and men's pleated crotches. Fur coats shone, pearls and gold were complimented relentlessly. Many smoked, awaiting the climax of the lengthy service.

I made my way into the foyer past banks of candles and cash-filled donation trays, through clouds of perfume and cologne, picked my way around mini gossip conventions and past gesturing hands crusted in diamonds, glistening lipstick, slicked-back hair, and mirror-polished shoes. I wondered what all this glitz had to do with the Resurrection.

My foot pressed into the soft red carpet as I entered the sanctuary of the Greek Orthodox Cathedral. I looked back and noticed that my shoe left an imprint, something my skills could not yet hide. The place was packed, and the crowds were murmuring. I saw an opening in the first pew and was bold enough to make a move. Sitting next to a round old lady dressed in black from head to toe, my eyes met the tired peaceful eyes of the icon of John the Baptist. The insectlike chatter became one big auditory fog, an incoherent static. I quieted myself, staying still in my own space, letting the intonations of the cantors leak into my ears.

The depiction of St. John was mosaic, made up of thousands of little pieces of colored tile. His hair was long, longer than mine; the serene man was dressed in loosely draped animal skins. His beard was knotted, and a halo of white light encircled his head. The Baptizer looked nothing like the clean-manicured parishioners that night.

The gray-haired, cherubic lady next to me leaned over and whispered, *"Ayios Ioannis* is looking at you." Her smile squinted her little eyes.

I was happy that this person could see me. I began to put aside my initial judgments. The old lady was so full of joy in her worship that it made me excited for what was to come. At midnight the cathedral's lights would go out, and one flame, representing Christ, the True Light of the World, would spread the lighting of the great procession of candle-holders.

At last the service was underway. Hours of anticipatory hymns were sung before the lights, bank by bank, were extinguished, and everyone, for that brief interlude, was invisible in darkness. The building now had become the great tomb. Then a single light walked in darkness. The bishop, wearing a silver crown and carrying a golden staff, began the singing of the religion's most triumphant song. The single flame began to spread, illuminating the sanctuary, row by row.

✳   ✳   ✳   ✳

Time passed in short shuffling steps and I had to dismiss the notion of pushing the people who stood in front of me. When I stepped into the night air I was glad to breathe it in deeply. When my mother closed her car door, I had already found my way into the backseat.

"*Christos anesti,*" I said as non-threateningly as possible. It means *Christ has Risen.*

"*Haaaa!*" She gasped in shock, but recovered quickly. "*Alithos Anesti! Costa,*" she replied.

Dad replied identically, "*Alithos Anesti!*" *Truly he has risen!*

✳   ✳   ✳   ✳

The house I grew up in smelled of freshly-cooked food that late night. The party would be catered the next day at Alex's house, of course, but it wasn't Easter without the house *spanakopita;* a blend of feta cheese, fragile crust, spinach and butter.

The next morning I worked out in the shadow of a sweet gum tree. Things were coming full circle at that point, I thought. When I was ready, and freed from distraction, I rubbed my head and gave thanks.

William had told me before I last left him that, "True invisibility happens naturally, when a life form can surrender itself wholly, even if only for a short time, to the miraculous pattern of which we are all a part. From the blind spots, ten thousand eyes are watching."

From the kitchen window, with steaming mugs in their hands, I could see my two parents watching me. Then, their expressions became puzzled, and I knew they were doubting themselves. Before their very eyes, I had disappeared.

✳   ✳   ✳   ✳

Alex's house was in a different real-estate league then the one we grew up in. He lived with his wife and my nephews in a gated community. The privately-secured block of four houses looked over its own shared golf course. A bionics surgeon, a tax judge, a diplomat from the Russian Free States were all neighbors, and with their families, were among those invited to the gala event.

✳   ✳   ✳   ✳

George, my nephew, was seven, and opened the door along with his mother when I arrived. Our hosts were dressed in never-worn white. Embraces were offered all around. Hors d'oeuvres and questions followed me like a shadow. I fought the urge to become unseen. I met cousins and wives and husbands of cousins and little kids and a contingent of very old people. *When would Demetri appear?*

By the time lunch was ready, I felt a sense of accomplishment in the fact that I had dealt with it all quite well. I spoke to doctors about the merits of Chinese Medicine, to lawyers on the importance of liberal arts in education, and to my parents about their own prodigal sons who were probably celebrating the *Anastasis* themselves. I told them how we are all connected, and that there was a balance.

"You're right Costa, all things arranged by God," said Mom as she hugged me for the dozenth time.

As we approached the lunch table, a rich repast prepared for fifty people, the doorbell rang again and Wyeth joined the party with a bottle of tangerine soda in his hand. He was thinner. It had been a year of transformation for all of us. I knew he moved into a studio and must have gotten a promotion. He was greeting folks with gracious handshakes, and appreciating the situation he had walked into. He flattered the lady of the house with compliments for her choice of carpet.

Wyeth appeared in awe of the musical water fountain in the backyard, swaying back and forth, following sounds and painting patterns. I knew he had been using Synth. It's in the eyes. I stepped away from the table and spoke with him in the other room, knowing it would take a few minutes for those gathered to find their places. Ceiling fans went *whump, whump, whump* over our heads. We stood in front of the bar and I offered him a drink.

"Orange blossom sir, just throw some of this in with a shot of vodka."

Beer usually tasted bitter when on the powder.

"Hey Gus, you look good, thanks for the drink, delicious. You want a hit?" Wye retrieved the flat purple nautilus-shaped inhaler from his pocket after looking once over his shoulder. "It's new, unbelievable, this is the prototype for the shelf brand. Can you believe, it's better than Street."

Real Street Synth came in a baggy and ingestion method was user's choice. A cocktail of expensive anti-depressants, anxiety inhibitors, and mood enhancers were thrown together the same way meth makers cooked up over-the-counter stuff. The powder Wyeth used to pick up for me was clean and made with precision. Inhalers were designed to release just the right amount for the user to remain cognizant and functional.

I reached for it, no time for this discussion, and pocketed it quickly. "Maybe later Wye."

"Suit yourself."

Apparently Martha was doing well. Back in school, taking care of herself for a change. She really did deserve something better than I could give her.

Sipping on his drink, "Mmmm, delicious."

"Enjoy."

"You enjoy yourself. That stuff I gave you is five times the price, five times the strength, and ready for market."

Why did he so easily give it to me then? I always guarded my stash carefully. I took hold of his elbow as he walked away. He turned, wrapping his cup in a paper napkin.

In all the years I knew him, it was the silence in our conversations that said the most. So I never asked him where he scored the drugs. Never bothered. He picked up, I got high. Now I wanted to know, and a suspicion that began to fester was as spooky as hearing your own voice on a recording for the first time. It was always there for others to know, but you never really knew until that moment. "Wye, who's your connect?"

Silence. A sip. Slowly retracting his elbow. "C'mon Gus. You know Alexander is a visionary. He knew it would be mainstreamed, FDA approved even. His guys have been selling powder forever.

The thump of the ceiling fans filled the pause.

"I thought you didn't want to talk about it," Wyeth frowned.

Whumpf...whumpf...whumpf...went the spinning blades.

"It's all right Wye, I'm just playing. I actually don't usually like talking about it."

His eyes got big with his smile. He was watching the fountain cascade and become a burning pink.

A fork in the other room clinked against a crystal glass. The prayer was about to begin. The grandmothers we call yiayias would lead the ceremony. Both older ladies were feeling the lightness that forty days of abstinence from liquor, meat, sweets, oils, and bad thoughts brings. Yiayia Cast asked those around the massive table to pray for all those who suffer, who lack faith, and who are lost. "May all my sons be brought home one day, and may Christ's gift be rejoiced today."

Looking at each other from across the table they sang the triumphant Resurrection Hymn. I observed the guests. The visitors were focused on the food, and were probably thinking about what they would say as they passed gravy or wine. They occupied themselves with anything but the day's true meaning. Servers stood respectfully at the periphery, their eyes meandering around the giant feast looking for openings to place more dishes.

The silence at the song's ending was beautiful, but was broken too quickly as chairs were pulled out, and rumps found placement on cushioned thrones. The furniture, Alexander explained, was made by the hand tools of Japanese carvers.

Nekros said hello with a passing pat on my shoulder. He and Serge were on the job.

Alex scanned the table for full glasses, and when it seemed everyone's cup was ready, rose for a toast. He nodded to his suited troll who held a black control box. Raising high his glass of red wine, the host shouted *"Christos Anesti!"*

The guests, beaming at anything the Ubermann might do, raised their drinks and replied, *"Alithos Anesti!"*

"Well, Happy Easter to you all," cried Alex, and thanks for joining our table. As you all know, I have been traveling, traveling into the future in a sense. I have met with Demetri's unit and am messenger of the good word that The United Free Balkans will soon be a reality!"

Glasses went up and baseball-fan hoots and hollers resounded.

Alex calmed the group with his own self-restraint. "This joyous victory comes along with the announcement of the birth of my own corporation. SynCorp will soon be a reality as well, providing stability and hope for the future."

He looked.

"We will be run from UFSA territory," he said, looking at his wife and gesturing, "ensuring that I will be home with family more often than not. So, with no further ado…"

He turned to an empty place setting, and on cue, a white-jacketed waiter respectfully filled the glass. Alex always planned ahead. I suddenly became conscious of many things.

"The hero of our family," Alex announced. "Let me introduce our final guest. My brother, Demetrios!"

Four projectors clicked on from each corner, and there, sitting in the perfectly placed seat, was Demetrios Cast. Wearing a blue beret and in full fatigues, he sat at our table with his hands in his lap, apparently awaiting some sort of cue to speak. Seconds later he began. *"Christos Anesti* from the soon-to-be United Free Balkans."

The whole party looked on in jaw-dropping awe. Georgey reached for him, and when his little hand passed through the image he began to cry. Alex motioned to his wife to pick him up.

Demetri sat quiet, waiting, almost as if he was squeezing himself into a small space. He spoke again. "It is late here, but those not sleeping have much company. The business of freedom does not go down with the sun. I thank Alexander and my company commander for arranging this visit. Although I will not be staying long, I would like you to know that I await the real reunion eagerly. I love you all very much, and implore you to celebrate well so that the freedoms we enjoy can be appreciated, and the sacrifices for those freedoms may not go unrewarded."

The image froze and Alex called us all to raise our glasses for Demetri, and for freedom. Mom and Georgey were both crying now, holding each other and being ignored by the group of hungry, excited guests. The soldier blipped into nothingness.

The ballet of spraying water could be seen performing through the great window behind Alexander. It abruptly changed directions and began to patter against the glass like on a windshield in a car wash. Alex turned around with a full mouth and gave the nod to Serge to fix it.

"I'll check it," said Penelope.

Alexander spoke to the stony bodyguard, "Well, I guess my wife wants to check it out."

I could see Nekros holding the hologram controller and wishing he could put it somewhere else while he too sunk his teeth into the tender roast lamb.

Wine got sipped, lips smacked, and the chitter chatter of a host of people began. It did not feel much like a family gathering, and the electric image of Demetri just made his being away seem more real. The water continued to rhythmically smack the window, and the lady of the house was outside in her bright white dress sleuthing around for the cause of the problem.

There were strange people having lunch with us. Besides the neighbors, there were slick business people, pharmaceutical reps, probably all tied in to the creation of SynCorp.

The fabric of the party was suddenly ripped by a terrified scream. The bubbling up of conversations fizzled and the smiles and excitement of salivary glands ceased. It was a woman's desperate cry coming from the living room. The fountain had returned to its normal elegance, but Penelope was still missing.

Many stood up so fast that some chairs actually fell over. Nekros and Serge were already there when I threw my awareness into the living room. Alex's wife was being thrust aside as Alex's two Special Agents sprang into action.

The assailant was revealed. Dripping wet, clad in black, his face covered in the ghastly laughing mask of a ninja demon. Nekros, quick on the draw, had his piece on target in a split-second. Serge shielded Penelope, also with gun drawn, and backed her into the dining room.

"Hands! Let me see hands now!" Nekros commanded.

I fully expected him to begin firing out of the sheer rage caused by this trespasser to his boss's house when he was on duty. The hands began to rise, but the permanent grin on the shiny red Oni mask foretold trouble.

"Kiaii!" shot from the assailant's mouth.

I staggered and felt shaky, like the first time catching a wave on a surfboard. Serge and Penelope actually fell, Nekros dropped his gun and wobbled. It was the Water-Word technique, the Mizu Ryu had returned. The mask's excited appearance was punctuated by two small horns atop the head.

This uninvited guest leapt from the ground, scissored Nekros's body, and hammered into the trained professional fighter with the accurately-delivered Full Of Water technique. The *Mizu-ga-ippai*, as the Japanese SAMs once explained to me.

The party screamed and howled, seemingly to the attacker's glee. Nekros's crotch became wet, and white liquid pooled on the carpet from his foaming ear. The assassin's masked eyes fell on Serge and his principle. Serge's pistol had fallen beyond his own immediate reach, and the killer stood straight as if goading him to go for it. Serge went, but quickly turned to charge the invader and take him hand-to-hand. As he entered the demon's space a small explosion went off, accompanied by a puff of thick, stinky smoke.

The guests screamed again, like excited sports fans. A gaseous gray blanket obscured all sight. Serge reeled backward from the cloud, clutching at his throat and colliding with Alex's neighbor. He rested permanently, death by crushed windpipe, and atop a crying surgeon who had always thought his Greek neighbors were crazy people.

Penelope had gone fetal in the corner and I could hear her whimpering. But the intruder didn't want her. I stepped up, now, and centered myself within the smoke screen. He had used the smoky cover to precisely strike and kill Serge, and now, in its opacity, he was coming for me.

I reached out with my senses. My ears caught a slight scraping sound. He was unsheathing a blade! I felt a change of air pressure, then a slight wind. My weight shifted to my back leg, my front leg ready to fire. My preparations came too late, he was already on me. pushing the blade against my lower rib cage.

The strength of the stab was incredible, and I heard something crack as I expelled air in a loud gush. But the blade did not enter my skin, my suit was made of cut-resistant fiber. I parried, pivoted, it was all just happening, the flow, what Candita had trained me for. Grab, but don't hold, attach while remaining detached.

He entered, I kept contact, parried, pivoted, flowed, my right hand reached my back pocket in search of a weapon. He slashed, and the suit saved me again, and then again. The crowd was panicking, plates were breaking, chairs falling. I heard my mother scream and I just kept fighting, maintaining balance, unbalancing him, until I had it, the hard inhaler, packed with Synth.

It was in my hand and my torso was wound like a spring from my reach-around. After achieving maximum torque, my spine twisted back and all my strength followed. The inhaler hammered and exploded under the chin of the red mask, tearing the murderer's disguise up and off. The strike sent a new cloud of once-condensed Synthetic Synergy into the air. The ceiling fans disseminated the purple powder.

The crowd gasped in unison as I held my breath as best I could. The unmasked demon rolled backward and ran for the window, his face matted in blood and powder. With a leap and a piercing fighting yell he shattered the window and landed on the front lawn. He bolted passed the fountain for the street. I followed with quick, calm steps.

I picked up a wooden cane that leaned against the wall at the house's entrance. With my enemy in the lead I eyed the ground for a projectile. My eyes found a white orb resting in a sea of green grass. In a single motion I grabbed and threw the golf ball. The long nights behind the bar, throwing darts and knives, had etched a technique into the memory of my throwing muscles. The ball cracked the skin on the back of the runner's head and stopped him in his tracks. The unmasked demon turned to face me, holding a bladed weapon that glistened in the noonday sun.

I stopped less than ten feet from my opponent, the separation of two fighters in a ring. But this was no competition; there would be no judges here today, no hero, either, to save my life from yet another mysterious killer.

He stepped forward, ignoring his injuries and the mind-altering effects of the powder plastered to his facial wounds. He raised the knife as I slid my hand down the cane to gain a better grip. In this calm state of hyper-awareness, part of my mind focused on the knife-wielder's face.

I recognized the dreadful face, the image that used to haunt my waking dreams: Tada! A bit older, but it was he. How? Cloning? Was he one of Japan's defensive weapons malfunctioning? Another shadowy experiment of war fallen into criminal hands? Perhaps now enforcing for a syndicate and trained in a modern ninja school, could he be a last attempt to secure the Synthetic Synergy market?

No. A soldier like this doesn't sell out to corporate money, and would never take payoffs from emerging pharmaceuticals like SynCorp. He simply did his job, or didn't come home. Tada sent his energy in a straight line, charging with everything he had, his blade aimed at my chest.

I stepped forward on a forty-five and met Tada's wrist with a hard downward strike from the cane, feeling the bone shatter. I moved again, this time with a thrust of the tip of the cane to Tada's midsection.

Sirens whined, indicating that someone in the party had the where-with-all to dial 911. As the defeated assassin deftly rolled backward, he removed an even more discreet blade from his black tunic. This hidden knife he plunged, in mid roll, into his own throat, granting him the same fate his twin had met over a year earlier—an honorable death by suicide.

$*$ $*$ $*$ $*$

By this time the party house was an asylum of disturbed and hallucinating people. The Suburban SAMURAI who arrived on the scene were having difficulty getting coherent statements, as I observed this meltdown from the cracked window. The new Synth pervaded the air and everybody's head. People cried, crawled, and grasped onto repetitive behaviors to stay sane.

A few were performing CPR and mouth-to-mouth, in a grotesque scene of chaotic tripping, to Serge's and Nekros's dead bodies. Some smoked, many just babbled a mile a minute about unimportant shit. Wyeth was mixing a drink and talking to himself. Alexander held his wife and children tightly, turning his head and looking around with paranoia in his eyes.

A few remained at the table and stared in awe at the hologram that had somehow been turned back on. The image was fractured, in fact headless. Words came with it, a steady monologue. I doubted it was Demetrios. Perhaps the satellite dish on the roof was picking up another reception. Or maybe the Synth had invaded my perception.

Whatever the case was, my attention was caught by the green glow. The quiet, gray-haired people looked on with me, as if seeing an unknown intelligent life form revealing itself with a "Greetings From My Planet—Take Me to Your Leader" speech. It was probably better then being fixated on the dead men in the living room.

Soft static was coming out of the surround-sound. I closed my eyes, taking my cue from the old folks. I reached into the crackle with my hearing and tracked what sounded like a human voice. "Gus…I must be tripping…Gus…."

The headless messenger was addressing me. I peeked with one eye.

"Gus…."

It had become a glow, a talking green glow, like some low-budget effect from the original Star Trek.

"Gus…I know this all seems too crazy to believe."

You're damn right, Demitch—crazy.

"Gus, you must listen to me. I am a seer for the military. A Remote Viewer operating in PsyCorp for USF Army–Eastern Europe. The future is not a precise science and I don't have all the facts. What I do know, what I've seen, is that you've got to find Basil. That's right, when you're ready, you're always welcome. Go seek it. May God be with you."

An empty chair. A crime scene, with dead people. Bewildered guests. I'm outta here.

Two tiny voices could be distinguished from all the mad babble in the room and in my head. The yiayias began to sing, slow and soft, but steadily strengthening. "To hold sand, one's hand must grasp lightly."

I actually smiled, and as I made my way on foot to the closest bus stop, I could still hear the yiayias, and a few guests, rejoicing in song, celebrating the Resurrection of the Savior.

CHAPTER 9

▼

TAKE ONLY PICTURES

Restless to wander
but where will I go?
If all is lost anyway
why not go slow
with water
and wine
and seeking the divine
smelling the people
who some think are friends
loving the people
because you just don't know when
those friends will be strangers
like Albert Camus
inhaling the world
but rejecting it too
and if all is lost anyway
why not go slow?

I focused on my breathing, filling my lungs with air and exhaling evenly the whole way back home. My rib was throbbing, but not broken. I had made it out of Jersey and out of suburban chaos. I wasn't much worried about the law, I didn't do anything wrong. Just reacted. They'd cover for me. Bobby once told me that Alex had more juice with cops than the mayor had. Besides, I'm invisible now.

- 81 -

82   Naked Among the Tombs

Stepping off the bus and into the electricity of Times Square at night stirred some old sensations. Advertising was everywhere, filling psychic gaps with naked images. People tend to seek an energy that is complementary, as water seeks its own level. I pressed on and found the round orange sign for the underground D train. It would rattle and roll me uptown to The Gym, where I could seek refuge in the old Dojo.

*   *   *   *

Slipped my shoes off in the dark. Paused and bowed ritually before stepping onto the mat. My toes gripped the canvas with each step. I walked deeper and deeper into the fatigue that follows high adrenaline. I removed the short sword from the wall. I pressed my back against the paneling and slid to the floor. Beneath the two masters' portraits, I clutched the *wakizashi* as a child might a favorite doll. The litany of invisibility began. Muso stepped into my still-warm shoes.

Fireworks burst behind my eyes. I sat still and meditated. Patterns swirled, dancing, mating, spawning. The simple beauty seemed inexhaustible. A cool breeze roused me, and I awoke in my skin. I fought the desire to analyze what had taken place at my brother's house. Three men were dead. I just wanted some tea, and a friend; a friendly cup of tea. I knew madness could be a few spinning spirals away.

The cat was tangible. This animal had kept my company often this year. We had the unspoken connection of some lost language. The cat and I shared the dignity of squatters, night walkers who sleep in small rooms.

I observed Muso stretch spine, claws, and mouth before heading for the door. Kitty was on the prowl. I followed quietly, hugging the sword to my body, slithering and changing form. I was as supple as elastic. The cat paused on the cold stone stairs frequently, sending his awareness from the refuge of corner shadows. He led me all the way down, to the clammy place beneath the basement cinderblocks.

We both peered into darkness for what seemed like several minutes. To my amazement Muso ran and leapt into the dark wall beneath the final bit of staircase. I moved fast, as fast as the cat, and found that my charging hand did not meet with hard, cold wall. Instead of obstacle, I found emptiness. The opening was masked in the darkness of shadow and had created the illusion of solidity. After my hand probed, my head followed. My body moved serpentinely into the shoebox-size doorway. My hands and beard made first contact with a thick Arabian carpet.

I smelled a sweet fragrance that I could not recall ever having experienced before. My adjusting eyes saw that the space was dimly illuminated by a candle's flame. Slowly I wormed in. More slowly still I stood. Muso's fur rubbed by me as he exited the discovery he had shown to me. I looked back at the tiny entrance door, then scanned the room and was astonished.

An altar, similar to the setup in my bedroom, yet larger and more ornate, stood three feet high against the wall farthest from me. The candle flickered from atop this stand revealing a depiction of a Shinto deity painted with Buddhist elements. It displayed a strange-looking blend of Japan's older religions. I could make out the figure; I recognized it from books. The deity hanging above the shrine, even though it held a staff and not a sword, and bore a shaved monk-head instead of Samurai style hair, was clearly, based on my literary explorations, the ancient god of war, Hachiman. The room's corners were bathed in pitch-black shadows, but gave off a strange energy. Suddenly, to my great gasping shock, a man stepped forward from the left flank.

I inhaled and pursed my lips to breath out. My heart began a war dance. When looking at this possibly spectral form I thought of holograms, and Synth, and anything logical that might explain this. The door was so small. The room so claustrophobic.

In the retro spectrum of all my other hallucinations, it always seemed better to be logical during a moment of unreality. Perhaps the dream inhibitors of my central nervous system had shut down, and this was all just a waking dream. But then, how much else of my life, even all the boring stuff, was just that—a dream?

The form before me was a healthy older man, an octogenarian with silver hair pulled back tightly in a ponytail. His teeth were straight and white. They gave him the appearance of being a devilish gentleman. The man wore skirt pants that tied up high on his waist. The traditional clothing was *hakama*, designed to allow for ease of motion while masking one's footwork. His hands were at his sides, and he carried himself with an aura of self-control.

His skin was brown and leathery. He bowed slightly, keeping his palms against both legs as his head dipped downward. Resuming his upright posture, he addressed me in a strong, even tone:

"Welcome *kohei*, your dedication to your training is praiseworthy. The paupers of the *Mizu-ryu* could not put you down. The next assassin they send will be a true killer. At your present stage, you will not even hear him coming before you are broken like clay and scattered to the wind like dried mud. You have yet to enter into the secrets. Kneel now, and begin the lesson of the Nine Hands Cutting.

I did what he said. Settling myself into a formal kneeling position, I straightened my spine and readied myself for knowledge. The Sensei cleared his pant leg with a sweep of his hand, creating a crisp sound. The specter knelt an arm's distance from me. I waited in a mixed state of amazement and primordial fear.

"The great master Zhang Dao Ling taught Zhuge Liang, the master strategist of the Three Kingdoms, the art of war. Zhuge Liang rose to become one of China's greatest tacticians. I will transfer to you the hand signs and power sounds of the master's lineage. The footwork remains hidden. With the footwork, this becomes a powerful defense that can protect your body from harm."

That last statement altered my awareness. It didn't wake me up, but made me aware that I was in a dream state. I was skating on the periphery of consciousness, and had the eerie feeling that I had heard all this before. This was a lesson being revisited. This was a scene I had acted out over and over again, but had no waking memory of. My instruction continued:

"The method is the Qixing Bufa, the Seven Star Method. If you learn the signs, sounds, and footwork, you combine heaven and earth. If you master this method completely, you will become an immortal."

Now I knew: this teacher was Pasito. His picture hung on the wall upstairs. I knew that he had been dead for years. Candy had called him a magician.

Pasito's smile stretched again across his face and the flicker of candlelight upon his brow revealed a man who could both inspire great respect and pose potential threat. I listened attentively, maintained breath control, and made every effort to learn the dead man's lesson.

I knew that in theory, an enlightened person's hands would naturally form into the mystical insigne that I was going to be taught. It is believed that when one reached a certain level of training, the hands automatically form the finger-locks in times of contemplation or stress. A part of me told myself that I was not ready. An ego self was flattered by the gift.

"*Rin!*" Sensei's voice came out guttural, called from his center point. Middle fingers interlocked and extended with their tips touching. This was the symbol of Strength.

"*Rin!*" I repeated from the recesses of my deepest gut and mimicked the hand posture. The yiayias, singing quietly, whispered in my inner ear.

"*Kyo!*" was transferred next. The leathery skinned index fingers extended and middle fingers curled around each other while the other digits remained interlocked. *Kyo* gives the ability to redirect the flow of energy within the body.

"Kyo!" I sounded out and relocked my hands. I remembered Tommy Ringle, and the feeling of water gliding over my skeleton.

"Toh!" This provided a harmony that animals could sense, and was represented by the pinkies and fourth fingers touching tips.

"Toh!" Muso's face popped into my mind's eye. It was imposed in front of the naked helix formed by my and Candy's bodies intertwining.

"Shah!" The index fingers extended and the other fingers interlocked. *Shah* symbolized the power to kill and restore life.

"Shah!" Tada's mad eyes stared through my new hand sign.

"Kai!" Pasitos's hands clasped each other with all fingers interlocking. This was the calming sign, and develops premonition of danger.

"Kai!" William's initial meeting with me, did he know the future that day?

"Jin!" represented knowing the thoughts of others by pointing the fingertips down while interlacing all fingers.

"Jin!" I felt that I knew what Martha was thinking, so long ago, in that hospital, without having to speak.

"Retsu!" is the mastery of time and space displayed by curling the fingers of the right hand around the extended pointing finger of the left hand.

"Retsu!" made me reexperience forgotten moments when I sat in meditation, holding eternity within an hour.

"Zai!" allows one to attain true invisibility and embrace the flow of nature. *Zai* is made manifest in the Thousand-Petal Lotus gesture, where the tips of the thumbs and pointing fingers touch and the extended palms face out.

"Zai!" I repeated as I sent my awareness out to the other darkened corner of the room.

"Zen!" had the Sensei touching thumb tips, and the right fingers were cradling the left fingers with the knuckles facing out. This was the symbol for ultimate bliss. Where yesterdays are never regretted and tomorrows are never expected. It was the symbol for being in the here-and-now.

"Zen!" I spoke with a calm strength, and saw myself telling William's story to listening children.

We both shut our eyes and placed hands on laps to rest and reflect. In this reflection, which seemed outside of time, the true *Kuji-Kiri* could be realized.

Suddenly, without warning, the Sensei was up and at attention. My eyelids dropped sweat as they came open. The perspiration was cold, yet feverish. My heart raced in my new understandings. The corner of the room began to emanate a hot breeze, and I stared into its lack of light with horror tingling my skin. I squeezed the scabbard until my knuckles were white.

A slender-figured man stepped from the shadow. The Sensei prostrated himself with his right hand extended toward the shadow-man, his calloused palm facing up. In this deep and formal bow, the spirit of the Sensei announced,

"O Sensei Hachiman, Oyabun and Shogun; sumimasen, kore wa Cone-Stan-Teen desu." The courteous specter of Pasito then stepped back to the darkness he had come from.

The Lord Hachiman stood in wait of my reaction. The highly thermal presence was dressed in a sea-blue kimono. Thin wiry muscles mapped his skeleton. His jet-black hair hung loosely and partially covered his face. A piece of his left pinky was missing. Any exposed body skin was colorfully tattooed. He was the mysterious drawing that hung on the dojo's wall.

I sank down slowly, put my right knee to the ground and pointed the sword's handle toward the floor. I spoke to the supernatural being in my best basic Japanese,

"Oyabun. Sumimasen, watashi wa Gus desu, dozo yoroshiku."

"Dozo-yoroshiku Gus-san," was the deity's pleased reply. He continued, "You have noticed my physical characteristics intently and see me as a gambler, a *yakuza*? Who I am is Lord Hachiman, the god of war. Your people once knew me as Aries, then as Mars. I am still the everlasting badge of blood in the sky! There is a battle going on, warrior, and I implore you to choose to walk in your Sensei's footprints."

As Hachiman finished speaking, the Sensei stepped out from the corner and into visibility again. Both beings overwhelmed the energy of the room, and I felt true terror move through me.

"Sacrifice is necessary for greatness, student," said the silver-haired master. "Now finish the lesson and kill yourself with that *wakizashi* blade and become an immortal Ninja in service of my honorable boss."

In disbelief of my own actions, but under some otherworldly control, I pulled the blade from the scabbard, one hair width at a time. I was mesmerized by the presence whose strange heat was lulling me into passivity. My sleepiness was slapped away in an instant when the growl of the cat Muso awakened me. *"Grow-wwl...!"*

My mind flashed to the poet Basho's words that were etched in gold calligraphy on a rusted sign in the dojo's bathroom:

I seek not to walk in the footsteps of the masters,
I seek the things they sought.

Me, Gus Cast, seeker of martial knowledge, became wide-awake and slammed the blade back into its cover. The action crushed the meat of my own hand and triggered a sensation of warm blood dripping into my palm.

The Sensei grabbed for my wrist with a grip of cold iron. Strangely enough, the more effortlessly I moved, the harder it was for him to hold me. The cat stuck one open-clawed paw into the room and growled again. I dropped to my belly and began the slow, wormy exit. As I stared into Muso's eyes, gaining strength from the yellow orbs, I could hear the Sensei scream,

"That blade you hold was used by me in this very same ceremony! This is a great honor!"

My bare feet finally pulled through and out of the hidden room. The cold touch on my feet bottoms sent a chill of ice through my centerline and spirited my escape toward my sleeping quarters.

∗   ∗   ∗   ∗

I ran as fast and sure-footed as Muso, barely making a sound up the winding steps. I snatched up my gym bag and loaded it quickly with a water bottle, some extra clothes, and a few old paperbacks. I turned and emptied my tip jar and jammed the crumbled currency into my pockets. When I turned back to grab my makeshift luggage, the orange cat had added himself to its contents.

"Muso, do you wanna come with me?"

The cat meowed and calmly met my gaze with an unconditional expression that reminded me of William Ringle. On my way out of the room I yanked down the old postcard I've held onto for so long and mixed it in with my money.

The Gym's doors exploded open, and Muso and I stopped and bowed to the school's entrance before hitting the cool city night running. I left the Bronx Gym and found my way into the subway, then through the Port Authority's haunted halls, and in line for a bus ticket headed West.

CHAPTER 10

▼

RUNNER, DIGGER, LISTENER

Sunday
is a writing day
I will release
the bright star pen
the bench
the punishment
the psychic when
it all came together
stepping Zen
No-mind
is your mind
the smoke dancer
the hen
that attacked the rooster
over and over again
I put the knife to it,
the rooster,
way back when,
after hanging it upside down
I took hold of its head
and pulled the dull knife back

and forth over and over and
over again.
The magic of the night is
walking into it
when
the world becomes art
and a paintbrush a pen.

The bus groaned and growled in waking up. Its passengers waited in dark, late-night silence to fill its belly. Half the tip jar money went for the one-way ticket. Adventure seemed like a worthwhile investment. I was able to put the recent past behind me so that I could experience the tinges of excitement in embarking on a two-day journey.

While waiting for the silver doors to open I set the gym bag down, folded my arms over my chest, and let my upper body hang forward. My spine gently popped and my hamstrings stretched. It was as if my body acted alone, in anticipation of the long, cramped ride. As I stood erect again, the blood flowed down in a big red wave of light-headedness.

On the doorway of freedom. Homeless and ready to wander. I let my self become a conduit for energy. I was ready, prepared for this moment. Strong, detached, capable. And empty.

The energy moved through me. The tingle intensified low in my back. I understood the life of the vagabond in this one pleasurable wave of self-controlled letting go. All the holy moments that awaited me. The eternal sunsets watched from freight trains, and mountaintops, and vast beaches. I almost felt guilty. One of these experiences could shake anyone from quiet desperation.

Before the doors could be closed a robotic canine came in to do a once-over. Passengers were already squirming and taking off layers of clothes, squishing pillows into arm rests, and fingering snacks. Most ignored the sniffer's patrol. Schnauzer-size and dull gray, these mechanical dogs appeared anything but menacing. Their programming supported their harmless demeanors. Asimov's standards safeguarded people from any harm, and relegated the robots to high-tech tattle-tellers.

Although this mechanical mutt could not intentionally hurt any life form, even frisky felines, I still secured the cat in my lap, and with mild interest observed the electric detective. Its jaw opened and closed, sending out inaudible sonarlike barks as it perused the aisle. Within the gun-sniffer's head was the capability to read a returned sonar image, cross-reference it with a ballistics and firearm database, then trigger an alert to summon the SAMURAI, with urban warfare capability, if necessary.

I once thought of robot-dogs as a natural evolution from remote-control cars and self-guided vacuums. Now, as I watched the toylike cop's photographic eyes extend and descend, I knew this was no toy, but rather an effective weapon in the international war to reshape society.

The trip began with the vehicle carrying half its capacity. Myself and two dozen others were flowing through the tree-lined roads of Pennsylvania. Muso and I felt like napping. Staring out at the early morning landscape lulled me into unconsciousness.

With sleep I entered an unusual dream state. The world behind closed eyes was the same as the world my body slept in. So identical was my mind's world to my body's that I began to feel as if I had become a ghost, an unseen spectral form that was observing the vessel that carried Muso and me toward Utah. The world was completely devoid of color, and my dream self watched all the other sleeping passengers. I noticed a breeze moving a lady's hair and pushing open the fabric of a fat man's shirt. The bus world was virtually without activity, save for the driver who steered the great automobile.

Then I was becoming aware of something else, something not seen only felt. A presence was around me. It gave me an icy chill that climbed my backbone like a mouse on a wire. My breathing altered. The presence grew more powerful by the second and the breeze began to tickle my beard. My heartbeat quickened as I looked at my own unconscious body and leapt back into it in hopes of finding shelter from this potentially dark force.

Upon entering my material self I was instantly aware of a choking grip on my throat. I had learned how to breathe through a choke. Short huffing breaths were my only defense against invisible hands that were relentless in their attack and inhuman in their strength. I suddenly knew that I had to wake up, if I didn't wake up I was going to die. Realization of my own mortality, not just knowing I would someday die, but feeling that death was actually upon me, frightened me even more.

If only I could scream—awaken the others and then they might wake me. If only I could move. Paralysis stopped me from even twitching a finger. I struggled and cried inside, and begged for strength to move a finger and scream any old sound in order to escape the icy hands that were ending my life. All I had, every ounce of fighting spirit went forth when I made the decision to die fighting this evil presence. My eyes opened and the sensation of surfacing after nearly drowning overwhelmed me.

"Hugggghhh," I gasped, and felt the cold dampness of my shirt and skin. What freed me from my fatal dream, I did not know. This did not seem like the place to diagnosis my disorder. It was necessary now to treat the symptoms and not fall asleep again. At the next stop I was going to fill my bag with high-energy drinks and pick up a snack for Muso. The cat had remained sedate and peaceful while sitting in the lap of a dying man.

*　　　*　　　*　　　*

Scanning the passengers, I saw that, like the relaxed creature in my bag, nobody else was aware of my black-and-white night terror. The bus was a microcosm of the country's lower middle-class population, myself included. There was no recorded yearly income for me, and I appeared on the government registry as a full-time student. Odds were that there were a few law-breakers and registry-dodgers on board. I felt akin. It's a good feeling, to be outside the Kingdom, or System, that marginalizes personalities and squashes individuality, all for the sake of security.

To travel two days on a bus was to learn about the silent majority without pie charts and statistics to dehumanize issues. The ride was reality, in-your-face America, and I could choose to shut down and try to sleep again, or engage my fellow beings and practice the humanism that so many religions spout out but turn their heads to when the sweaty crack of their fellow American's ass almost touches them as they bend to pick up the quarter they dropped, or a baby's crying from the seat behind them turns tortuous, or listening to their heartfelt beliefs seems ignorant or stupid.

The bus's air brakes squeezed out an *"ooosh"* sound, signaling a refueling stop. "You got ten minutes folks!" the driver informed his groggy human cargo.

The fluorescent lighting in the restaurant/hardware store made the white countertops glow as most patrons wandered in, drone like, and squinted their way to the order counter.

I milk-and-sugared my cup next to a man I nicknamed "Legs." Legs wore all denim and was rail thin and very tall. His boots were beat up, black, military issue. Legs was missing a lot of teeth and chain smoked whenever the bus stopped rolling.

"Goin' far?" I asked.

"Just to Nebraska," replied Legs. "Decided to leave my rig at home and let someone else do the drivin' fer this one. 'Bout yerself?" he asked, smiling and revealing the big space where his six front teeth once were.

"Utah. I'm going to visit my brother."

"You-all Mormon?"

"No, he went out there a while back. Worked for a Fresh Start program in the desert. I guess he liked it...the desert."

"Oh, Hoods-in-the-Woods type. Yeah, it's too bad those things got shut down once the wars started. Now dey just keep 'em locked up or get 'em into the Service. I was in the Service; my nephew, he's locked up."

*   *   *   *

Talking with Legs opened up my awareness to the cast of characters with whom I traveled. Joseph and Mary sat in front of me, fundamentalists who got a huge kick out of telling people their names. The two were newlyweds who thumped the Bible for fun and talked about the end-time as if it were already upon us.

Gambler Mike had won a large sum of money on an Internet gambling ring run out of Barbados, and he was going to try and be "the man," as he put it, one more time. The Dehydrated Kid laughed with cracked dry lips at Chief Dull Knife's jokes. The Native American jokester wore a jacket inscribed, Chief Dull Knife's Football, and after one-on-one conversations became group discussions, I found out that he was a representative from a native nation, going back home for "some tribal business." Tom Brooks, who sat alone next to the toilet, claimed to be a bounty hunter, and offered me a pull on his vodka bottle. I declined, but was curious as to whom he was going after.

"Ohhhh, now I just go after kids, runaways and such, git 'em drunk and laid one time before bringin' 'em in."

After more than twenty-four hours of traveling together, an undeniable exchange takes place between passengers, a change that five-hour shuttle-flight travelers will never experience. By the time we reached Iowa we had not only added people to our talking crew, but had become friendly enough with each other to discuss the topic that lay hidden on the back burner of many of our minds—apocalypse.

* * * *

Mary knelt on her seat and turned to look at me. Her speech, delivered in a quiet Southern drawl reminiscent of the little psychic lady in the film *Poltergeist*, was interspersed with direct biblical quotes, like,

> *"And the heaven departed as a scroll when it is rolled together; and every mountain and island were moved out of their places. And the kings of the earth, and the great men, and the rich men, and the chief captains, and the mighty men, and every bondman, and every free man, hid themselves in the dens and in the rocks of the mountains; And said to the mountains and rocks, Fall on us, and hide us from the face of him that sitteth on the throne, and from the wrath of the Lamb; For the great day of his wrath is come; and who shall be able to stand?"*

Almost on cue Joseph popped up and began to recite scripture, as well, like they were playing us with good cop/bad cop:

> *"And to you who are troubled rest with us, when the Lord Jesus shall be revealed from heaven with his mighty angels, In flaming fire taking vengeance on them that know not God, and that obey not the gospel of our Lord Jesus Christ: Who shall be punished with everlasting destruction from the presence of the Lord, and from the glory of his power."*

As the sermon finished, Joseph and Mary's eyes scanned the now-quiet listeners who were held in rapt attention. The couple settled on Dull Knife, who seemed to be suppressing laughter.

Knife erupted, "Don't look at me, I'm a Christian!"

Joseph and Mary looked at each other with concern, and Mary apologetically responded, "Oh, no, Mister, we don't mean to scare nobody, or pass judgment."

Dull Knife's face became serious. "Well, good, 'cause like I said, I'm a Christian...and a Buddhist, and a Muslim, and a Traditional Indian, and a Commie, and a Capitalist...and a...."

He could hold his act together no longer and burst into laughter followed by the kid next to him whose lip began to bleed down the middle in his wide-mouthed excitement. The two slapped five, and in between roars Dull Knife said,

"Why don't you drink some water, man? You're drier than the Mystery Whore of Babylon!"

94   Naked Among the Tombs

That final comment sent the whole group into an elated mood that did not end for quite a while.

*   *   *   *

Somewhere approaching Wyoming, the passengers drifted into unconsciousness, save for a few. I was anonymous and on the move. Traveling. Left three dead men in Jersey, being stalked by something nobody else could see. Doing anything to stay awake. Nothing to lose.

I spoke to Dull Knife. "You know, some believe that a lot of the ancient heroes, like Samson and Hercules, were masters of *chi*, as the Chinese call it, and because of their profound connection with the power source they were capable of superhuman things, even…immortality."

"What do you believe, man?" asked Knife.

"I think there's truth to that; but I also think that true heroes are not easily explained."

"There's a lot of unexplained things in that desert you're going to; it's an ancient home to many native people."

"Well, I'm just going to see my brother, Basil."

"That's it, huh? Well, I guess that's good enough, then. The Indian folded his arms and hung his head for a final nap.

"Hey," I continued. "What do you know about the desert?"

"I know that the Ute and the Paiute, and the Navajo, and the Fremont, and the Goshute people have always respected the Skin Walkers, and nowadays people don't. So, those who walk in both worlds are getting pretty pissed off."

"Hm. Skin Walkers?"

"Yeah, Skin Walkers. But don't be saying that name out loud down where you're going, even the white folk are superstitious 'bout it. Goodnight man, wake me up in Wyoming."

"Goodnight."

*   *   *   *

When we hit Salt Lake City, Tom Brooks, the bounty hunter, and myself were the only ones left from the original talking group. Because Brooks had a car waiting for him and we were both heading in the same direction, at least for a few hundred miles, I offered to pay for half the gas to tag along.

"'Course, Tom Brooks can use the company," was his answer.

Rolling down the window, I bathed in the freedom of the wind on my face, and saw it as a step closer to the true freedom of walking.

Things changed as we got farther south. Brooks got even more drunk, and the landscape got more magical. The high desert was closing in on us when the hunter's phone rang.

"Hello? Shit, I'm just coming from there...okay...be there in two hours or so."

Clicking his phone off, Brooks pulled over with a gravelly skid, looked at me and said, "Well, either you get out here, or ride back with me to Salt Lake."

Salt lake had appeared to me as a monolith of a city whose clean exterior must belie some darker secrets. Although it was the same state, and Basil probably wasn't going anywhere fast, the big city felt too distant from my brother .

"It's okay Tom, I'll walk from here. I've got plenty of water."

"Okee dokee. See ya, then."

A quick U-turn and his rear lights blinked away into nothingness. I was walking in twilight, heading south to a town called Ghostbead. As day fully rolled into night, I embraced the star-filled Utah evening. I walked and sipped water, thankful for finally being away from the vehicles that got me where I had to be.

More than two days without sleep and little food, combined with the exchange of stories and others' opinions and energies, made my experience highly surreal. I began to not care if it was all really just a dream. I let exhaustion become my reality, and when I did that, no longer felt the pangs of fatigue.

After several hours of walking in this dream world, embracing the eternal feeling of the giant night sky, a rumble of a small engine broke my reverie. Then a shot cracked the air, *"Baang!"*

Immediately squatting and making sure Muso was safe, I looked around with the eyes of a prey animal. I did not know how long I had been walking on this dirt road that was surrounded by Aspen trees. I cursed myself for losing the highway.

The engine was getting closer and I debated the functionality of invisibility when someone was firing a rifle into the darkness. Smaller firearms, like rifles, were still legal in rural areas; guns were tools for predator control. The shot was a quick and scary welcome into cattle country.

The engine was upon me. I put Muso behind me and raised both arms, making myself as big and visible as possible. I yelled out, "I'm a person! Don't shoot!"

The motor yawned into silence. Then came the high wattage beam that would temporarily blind and expose me.

"What the hell are you doin' out here?" yelled the armed four-wheeler rider, before squirting a generous shot of tobacco-saturated saliva onto the trail.

"Traveling. Going to meet my brother near Ghostbead!" I yelled back, with my arms still raised high.

"Shheeeeeet, Ghostbead? Let me guess, your brother is livin' in the Warren?"

With that response, and the spotlight going off, I began to feel there was hope, and maybe even luck, in my dreamlike evening wanderings.

Securing his rifle safely to the rack on the back of his four-wheeler, the rider approached me, spat, and shook my hand. "Name's Cowboy-Kid, I'm friends with the folks in the Warren."

I introduced Muso and myself. Upon seeing the cat, Cowboy-Kid said, "Oh, figures, you are headin' to the Warren, ridin' with a cat and all, sheeeeet."

"What are you shooting at, at this hour, Cowboy-Kid?" I asked, in a relieved-to-be-alive sort of way.

"Cai-oats! Still lookin' fer the som-bitch that ate my Achilles tendon."

I noticed his limp as he remounted his vehicle. After forty minutes or so of driving through puddles and over rocks, we parked at the Country Café in the small, one-restaurant-town of Ghostbead.

"I ain't takin' you out to the Warren now, a-course. In the morning I'll ride you out there in ma pickup," said Cowboy-Kid as we dismounted and approached the café's entrance. "You're welcome to my floor space fer the night."

"I really appreciate all your help, Cowboy-Kid. Just out of curiosity, any reason why you don't wanna go there tonight?"

"Git in dere, man, I'll till you 'bout it over some of Lulu's coffee."

✳   ✳   ✳   ✳

The café was small and had the air of an old saloon that had lost its liquor license. The place was loaded with people wearing six-gallon hats. The Kid's entrance was greeted with a few nods and hat tips. A TV mounted in the upper corner behind the counter blared war footage from all over the globe.

American flags, old and new, coated the walls, along with Marine Corps memorabilia. Sabers, cartoon bulldog heads, and the Latin phrase, Semper Fidelis, graced even the bathroom. Framed newspaper articles of Marine Corps medal winners, obituaries, and front-page VICTORY headlines appeared beneath the glass tops on round wooden tables. Lulu greeted us with a smile and a pot of coffee.

When our double order of bison burgers with fries floated over to the table, a heavily muscled man who was seated at the counter noticed us. This giant cowboy dismounted from his stool. After sending a quick watch-what-I'm-gonna-do chin wave to his friends, the behemoth approached. The man must have been nearly seven feet tall, a real giant with freakish musculature. A patch covered his left eye. He removed his black hat that bore the Corps' silver insignia, and a bed of straight blond nails seemed to be sprouting out of a skin-covered square.

"Evenin', Kid," he said, as his shadow fell upon this hungry and seemingly reluctant rescuer of mine.

"Evenin', Sarge," the Cowboy-Kid responded. He looked nervous as he squeezed ketchup onto the round, meaty delicacy.

"Who's yer new girlfriend? Where ya from, man? Or are ya just home from the jihad?"

I looked at the Kid for some response, but saw only closed-eyed embarrassment. I sensed he was waiting for Lulu to come to the rescue. It couldn't have come too soon.

"Now, Sergeant, couldn't you leave these boys alone, please? They are my customers, and in here, you must remember, I am the Commander-in-Chief." Her sweet, motherly voice and smile defused the situation.

The giant returned the good manners to the little lady and replaced his black hat onto his spiked flat-topped head. He departed our company with, "A-course Lulu, I'ze jes playin'. Y'all have a good night."

The two of us ate in silence, and I was tactful enough to not ask for an explanation until morning.

*   *   *   *

The Kid was surprised that a city-boy would wake up earlier than he did. The fact was, I had never slept. I meditated, and drank instant coffee, but I could not sleep. I was still too scared to let myself shut down.

*   *   *   *

In the two-hour dirt-road ride to the community he called the Warren, the Kid tried to explain things. His truck's cab was spacious and made conversation easy. I was glad to not be on the back of his quad. The pro-wrestler who had poked fun at me was a war hero. He had suffered devastating injuries battling

Holy Warriors, but returned to fight again and again in exchange for government-funded bionics. Steroids kept his muscles up to speed with his new parts.

The Sergeant was heir to King's Ranch, whose acreage bordered the community Basil lived in. On the ranch he practiced his own form of Mormonism. He had taken a new name for himself from his religion's holy book; Omni, and was a self proclaimed preacher. Everyone referred to him simply as Sarge. He identified his own group of veteran friends with the Navoon Legion. This Legion was the old militant branch of the original Latter Day Saints church. Sergeant Omni believed them to be the true heroes of the Utah-America war.

*　　*　　*　　*

The Warren's central barn was surrounded by yurts; round, tentlike structures with skylights. They looked planted. Their reddish-brown skin blended in with the earth and gave the whole area a tribal village appearance. The sturdy barn we parked in front of looked deserted. There was no sign of vehicles or even people.

"C'mon Gus, lazy dodgers are probably jist sleepin'," said the limping Kid before opening the door. Out of the corner of my eye, and only in my periphery, did I notice a shoeless man standing next to the still-warm truck. When I looked directly, the man was gone.

"Helloo, it's only me, and Basil's brother, Gus." Kid's voice expanded under the building's high ceiling.

Rows of bunk beds lined the tapestry-covered sidewalls, and a wood stove sat in the middle of a kitchen area at the far side. A curtained metal tub, like a prop in a western, waited patiently behind a curtain for trail-weary gunfighters to sink into. Glass oil lamps waited dormant for night to come. There were overflowing bookshelves surrounding the entrance that reached nearly to the high ceiling.

The floor was made of clean wooden planks. It looked like it was swept often. Dents and scratches abounded, however, and showed the building's use. The floorboards didn't creak at all when the person appeared behind us.

"Awwww...." She let out a catlike yawn. "Excuse me."

"Aaahh!" Cowboy-Kid screamed when he jumped and nearly stumbled over his straight leg. Regaining his composure he said, "I hate when you do that."

Rita embraced my jumpy Samaritan in a hug, looking at me with soft, amazed eyes. She hugged me also, and when her embrace seemed like it could no longer give any more welcoming energy, she said, "I'm Basil's partner, my name's Rita, and you look really tired."

＊　　　＊　　　＊　　　＊

Rita was olive-skinned and appeared to have stepped out of an icon. Her long fingers, almond-shaped eyes, and particularly Middle Eastern features, melted away any concern I had had for Basil's well-being.

Tara joined us next; an impishly short spark plug of a woman who fed me bread made from root flour. She served the simple meal with a lightly-fried sweet cactus. I sipped a Christmassy-smelling cold tea as Rita began to prepare a fire. She needed to heat enough water for the bath! What a way to greet an uninvited guest!

Basil was out shepherding with some of the other residents. The coyote population had grown so large recently that no amount of traditional predator control could keep the free-range cattle and sheep safe. My brother was following and making camp around the herds in coyote territory. Thankful ranchers paid him well in beef and bulk supplies, the currency that the Warren wanted.

Tara, her blue-black hair in braids, had a once-ivory complexion gone red in the sun. Her small bare feet seemed spring-loaded by the way she moved. She surprised me with the question, "Would you mind if I shaved you?"

Dreamy-eyed from good fortune and fatigue, and this lady's primal beauty, I replied, "Aahh…sure," without giving the left-field question a second thought. I gave a last tug on my scraggly facial hair.

She plucked a glass-textured black blade from somewhere, and I eyed it with curiosity. "It's obsidian. When knapped right, it can get much sharper than steel," my cheery barber explained. She pulled and gently scissored off and easily removed the hair covering my face before applying a thick lather. The stone-age tool moved over my face like a warm wash cloth, and left me with just a goatee. Rita, like a surgeon's assistant, handed Tara a jar of sage oil, which she liberally rubbed into my face and freshly manicured beard.

Rita prepared to stoke a fire with a process that pulled me back through time and left me speechless. On one knee, she spun a piece of wood that looked like a thick pencil wrapped in the string of a small bow. The spinning wood was capped by an animal's palm-sized ankle bone and drilled into a small board. The process created smoke, then a small orange ember, which she placed into a nest of dry tinder and blew into flames. Rita put the burning ball into the stove, atop which sat a large water kettle.

Soon I was lying back in the metal tub of steamy water. I seriously questioned myself as to whether I was dreaming. There were no clocks around to record the passing of time, only good solid things that were useful in and out of dreams. From a space in the curtain I could have sworn a man crawled from behind one of the colorful tapestries. I closed my eyes and let myself go.

Who cares? Who fucking cares anymore what's real?

I thought this to myself, and quickly slipped into a deep…deep…sleep.

CHAPTER 11

▼

CLAW MARKS IN THE SKY

Maybe today
I will not struggle
and freedom's sweet breath
will blow on my face.
I was hiding in
a library
and suffering
from what
I vaguely recall was
the greatest hangover
of them all...
Enlightenment came
into my shaky gaze
and dry brown leaves
covered my feet and scraped
as I walked
and I
alone
knew
in my heart of hearts
that microorganisms
from old books
had made their way

into my system
and my booze soaked brain
etherized
these invisible masters
of ancient secrets.
I have been sorting
the knowledge ever since,
but,
maybe today
I will not struggle.
Perhaps my gaze will be filled with the light
of wisdom
once again and
I will take my place
as The Spy in the House of Babylon.
Today, I will not struggle
for I have already
let go of the illusion.
Control is a dried leaflet
rolling toward the water.
The world beyond is just within
is the crux of this, this, memory
of that day, or days,
when I did not struggle
and freedom's sweet breath
blew on my face.

How did I get here? I wondered, before making the assumption that I had dozed off and they had somehow brought me outside. But my clothes had been changed. Maybe I was so spaced out that I had gotten up myself and just...,lost time. But people lose time when aliens abduct them, not when they travel to the desert to visit their brothers.

I was kneeling in formal *seiza* and waist high in slow-moving water. The sun was going down on a vast landscape made up of giant red rocks. Some of the stone giants looked like mud that had dripped from heaven—fallen from some ethereal sandbox, they had hardened to become silent shadow-givers.

The creek flowed steadily, and seemed to sing to me a song of eternal change. Its movements prodded me to tilt my head back and look straight up at acres of transforming sky. Brightness faded, and the great black cloth, full of holes, soon roofed the ceiling of our planet. I wasn't cold, sitting in that water, but my hands naturally came together and held each other, and my lips moved in quiet recitation of the ancient power sounds. The ten digits that fed me, clothed me, and touched the world, moved in accordance with the guttural resonance.

Rin...
Kyo...
Toh...
Sha...
Kai...
Jin...
Retsu...
Zai...
Zen...

My feet became alive. I rose to the balls of my pedals and into *hanza,* the readiness posture. The waters cascaded from the traditional Japanese clothing I wore as I rose to one knee. The fabric was heavy with the creek. Coming to full stance, I stepped from the water into the starry night.

The mighty Ursa Major was slowly circumnavigating Polaris, pointing the world north. The Big Dipper, the keeper of the seven-star mystery, nearly brought me to tears. I let the welling up become joy, and then motion. I moved, and the skirt pants hid my footwork. To my astonishment, I was performing the secret footwork. I had the signs, the sounds, and now the dance of immortality conveyed down by the constellation. My body became warm, and dried my clothing. The sandstone pillars, now bathed in moonlight, seemed to smile on me, and welcomed me to their world.

*   *   *   *

Muso walked by and dragged me with invisible strings. He pulled me toward a new location. After surmounting an embankment I became witness to an incredible and spacious canyon. Green light spilled in, and transformed the terrestrial orifice into a lunar landscape. My ability to deftly navigate in the cat's footsteps surprised me. We traveled down, moving like water. The scene we reached was more awe-inspiring then the hundred-foot drop we had descended.

A man wearing the orange robes of a Buddhist monk, shadowed by an over-sized straw hat, stood peacefully facing the Sensei and the god of war Hachiman. They were all still, waiting for me.

Muso took his place at the monk's side. Stepping forward, I became the median for these four characters. I could do nothing else but align myself. I had no interest in finding out what was going on, just being there was enough, and letting my essence conduct chi. I aligned, and automatically threw my awareness out like a fisherman casting a net. My eyes took in the scene with a wide-angle lens.

Now William Ringle stood where Muso had just crouched! He no longer appeared as a homeless vagabond, but instead wore the countenance of a very holy man. The figure in the Chinese hat tilted his head back to star-gaze and revealed himself as the Sifu Tommy. His gentle smile assured me that everything was as it should be. Pasito stood as motionless as cold steel. His master seemed to be hovering, almost imperceptibly just above the earth's surface.

*   *   *   *

The criminal lord Hachiman ended the portrait's stillness with a commanding *"Rai!"* that echoed around the canyon's walls. The Sensei of the *Kuji-Kiri* and his master bowed together. William and Tommy placed their right hands in front of their hearts and bowed in a similar show of mutual respect. All four stepped back and knelt formally, hands at rest in laps. A wind stirred and my attention was drawn to a patiently attentive animal audience atop the canyon's walls. Deer, coyote, rabbit, raven, owls and bears formed the watchers.

The spirit of the Sensei turned his eyes toward me and spoke.

"Tsuki o kaimasenka." He told me that they had offered me the moon. And in that one phrase let me know that I had gone from student to enemy.

"Watashi-no Oni!" He vehemently introduced his Demon!

The soil, the very earth before me rumbled and became animate. A figure rose from the red sand. It solidified, evolving from loose dirt into a stone statue. What took the desert towers countless years to do, this silent gholum did in seconds. The red thing opened its eyes beneath its helmet and stared coldly into my core. It wore two swords on a black belt and was heavily armored, like a feudal warrior of old. The newborn monster was garbed in a sunburned plate-mail black gear. It uplifted its red palm and bowed like the Sensei had done before, an obedient gangster in the service of an overlord. Returning to attention, the shadowy figure awaited a command.

"Rai!" shot again from Hachiman's mouth. This time the command was aimed at me, and the sandman, who I realized was to be my opponent. We were being told to bow to each other. Then the call to arms came: *"Hajime!"* The macabre swordsman drew his blade.

I somehow remained calm. Fear was present, in every cell of my body, but wasn't going to skew my abilities. I stepped and raised my hands to my center. The warrior belched out a war cry and I felt it in my *dan-tien*. My center point fought back. A sword was stretched from its casing and cut the air near my ear, and I realized the horror and wonder of the situation that was upon me. I was able to admire the beauty within this murderous act. The sound, and the power, and the exhilaration of a stage in my existence coming to an end had a remarkable aesthetic that I was able to recognize.

I was unarmed, but suddenly ready to engage this underworld creature's deadly dance. The black knight recovered from his failed attempt to disembowel me and was attacking again. But I could not be touched. My body floated over the rough ground. A seven step pattern saved me from oblivion. I performed the mystical fighting form unconsciously. Then, when I knew I could skate forever, and that it was impossible for this opponent to make contact with me, I just as effortlessly decided to end it. Before he struck again I let my knees bend slightly, felt my pelvis push forward, and allowed my head to lead my spine in straightening.

My hands rose to eye level and I showed my opponent the power of The Thousand-Petaled Lotus. The animal audience up top became excited, and shuffled feet and paws and talons. Little rocks felled bigger stones. Avalanches formed against the canyon walls. As the warrior swung I grounded myself, determined to remain motionless.

The sharp-looking blade entered my body's space and disappeared into a vortex of concentrated energy. The weapon phased through time and space as I had willed myself to become my own natural spirit form. It remarkably met its end in the dark knight's own throat. The powerful strike, which passed into a piece of folded universe, dismembered him instantly and the helmeted head crashed to the ground. The body, like a cut-through tree, surrendered to gravity as well and came down with a crash. The face-plate popped open on the helmet and the Red Demon of my worst waking nightmares stared ghoulishly into nothingness. The

106   Naked Among the Tombs

crowd of on looking creatures roared! Howls, growls, hoots, and caws filled the ancient moraine.

Sensei Pasito, the headless sword demon, and Hachiman—the lord of man's battlefields, vanished instantly. They left no evidence of their presence or existence.

*   *   *   *

Like a gladiator I looked up toward the balcony crowd. Things had changed. People stood and kneeled where animals once had crouched and perched. They had shifted, just as Muso had become William. They were aglow with youthfulness and rejoicing in this victory over darkness. The crowd were natives to the earth, dressed in roughly hewn hides and furs and blending in with the environment of rocks and sand and sagebrush.

William and Tommy placed their hands at their hearts and bowed toward me, their student. After returning the act of respect I smiled at these two vessels of purity who had escaped suffering, and must have chosen to return to the world as Boddhisatva, or maybe even as Boddhidharma himself. Perhaps they had returned from eternal bliss to guide me to this moment.

The young people cheered again, and charged down the canyon's walls. Rubble and dirt careened toward the creek bed. The group met in the water, became calm, and waved me in. I joined them and knew to stand, then knelt near the one who had watched my fight through the eyes of a great bear. The bear-man cradled my head with his hands and dipped me backward. From a lens of smooth flowing water I could see the great growing ladle. I could hear the words:

> *"Holy Ghost Power protect you!*
> *Holy Ghost Power keep you!*
> *Holy Ghost Power guide you!"*

Then a rush of air, and a returning.

*   *   *   *

"I think he's coming around," was what I heard from a place between flesh and spirit. Hands touched my head and torso. The wood floor lay beneath me. A towel was draped over my crotch. The one remaining element from the desert battleground was my baptizer's blessing.

"Holy Ghost Power make you awake!"

*   *   *   *

"Gus! C'mon man, Gus, you did it, now you can come back to us."

This voice was as refreshing as it was familiar, and it was as familiar as my own blood. I coughed out bath water, closed my eyes, and composed myself.

Then it was my turn to speak. "Basil, it's nice to see you."

This is all I said after returning from a place whose description seemed beyond my language. I was wet and naked, and must have appeared somewhat infantile after being pulled from possibly drowning in a bathtub. I did not feel awkward or embarrassed, though. Basil and his friends made me comfortable, and gave me the unlikely impression that everyone who visits might go through the same thing.

I sat up and noticed that the three who were chanting about the Holy Ghost took off in what I thought were animal like bounds. They disappeared behind the tapestries. Maybe the last cob webs of dream time had vanished with them.

Basil did not have long dreadlocks covering his face. He did not wear the mouth-hiding beard of a hobo squatter making it out west. The look of what I once thought represented anarchy and revolution was anything but what he surrounded himself with. His short hair was combed to the side and peppered ever so slightly with the gray streaks of time and responsibility. A mustache sheltered his upper lip, and made me think that he was undercover as a cop, an old-school detective who locked up the people who were like he, himself, used to be.

The eyes were his, though, they belonged to my family line, and every Cast had them—sleepy and watery at times, old, in an old-soul sort of way. I stared and he smiled back. He touched my city-skin, which was pale, but had been thickened from scraping ring canvas and rubbing against padded gloves. Basil's hands felt gloved by the calluses of outdoor life. His skin was brownish leather.

Comfortable clothes, tasty food and warm hugs were passed around generously.

My brother smoked a pipe and drifted around, always smiling, and often fielding quiet questions. I could see him nod "Yes" to an odd looking fellow wrapped in a blanket and who stayed hidden beneath a hood.

Rita and Tara and several others were sincerely interested in the journey, and the cat I carried with me, and who I, Gus Cast, actually was. I felt quite exhilarated to be in the center of everyone's attention. Still, I observed Basil, and the hooded figure, and the glint that came from the sunglasses he wore. The shadowy visitor who spoke with Basil was wearing sunglasses after stepping into the barn from the dark of night. My brother looked at me looking at him and patted the mystery man on the shoulder before he walked away from us.

I knew he was thinking that I was very welcome when he contentedly puffed his pipe. I wondered if I was truly ready for our reunion, and the new experiences that might come with it.

∗   ∗   ∗   ∗

Tara had been a school teacher before her discontent had become too great to bear. She said that the classroom, like the society that built it, had become spiritually dead. Tara believed that in nature, in the wilderness, the truth of life would come shining through, as clear as a crack vile glistening on the public school's lawn, as clear as the bottled water she used to bring to work because of the brown, brackish stuff the school's tap spewed out. The years she had been around Basil and the other friends of the Warren proved her beliefs to be correct. She also said that, like everyone else around, she had found this desert sanctuary through a series of coincidences. This added to the idea of the community being the right place to be—on all levels. She seemed to like it when I jabbered on about chi energy and other martial arts topics.

"You know Gus, its not just people, or even animals, who conduct the Life Force." She made this statement while rubbing tension from my shoulders.

I tugged thoughtfully at my newly trimmed beard and cleared my mind before responding with, "Like plants and insects?"

She answered, "And rocks, and water, and all things, Gus."

The floor of the huge, warm barn was dotted with small groups of people having conversations. One guy was picking at guitar strings. The energy was excited, yet mellow. Every time I made eye contact with someone I received a friendly smile and nod.

Where was Basil? Just as I thought it, a pile of soft, brown material fell into my lap. There was my brother, hovering over us, pipe clenched in his teeth and arms akimbo.

"Rita and I made 'em."

They were moccasins, tall ones that tied just below the knee.

"Thanks."

"Don't thank us…seriously, we had fun making 'em. The deer, she's the one to thank."

They smelled of wood smoke and were so soft I just wanted to rub my face in them. The mocs were going to help me feel the earth. They tied in the back so they wouldn't snag anything.

When I first wore them I felt like I had been given new feet. I stood with my new feet on, and noticed that everyone was lining up and filing out through a hole in the wall, which had been covered by a cloth. Basil held it up, his pipe gone and his eyes on me again.

The long, dry tunnel led to corridors. There were intersections along the way. No one spoke, just crawled. The occasional beam of red flashlight exposed roots and earth. I understood my hosts' discipline of silence. This place was called the Warren.

Our mother had read to us as kids about rabbits. We both dreamed of being like the heroes in the book, always running, digging, and listening. One day, we thought, we would each become, somehow, like the great rabbit myth, a prince with a thousand enemies. Perhaps that romantic day was almost upon me. After all, the police might be looking for me. I did abandon my life. Dropping out of the System is bound to piss someone off.

Just as my anxiety began to rise, a palm of a gentle hand pressed against my forehead and slowed down my body and mind. It let me know that everything was going smoothly. The person up front exited through a partially-rooted sage-brush door. The plant held strong connection deep into the tunnel. I watched Basil spit water on the woody veins. He then patted its tentacle gently with a handful of soil. The one up front looked around and crept out with slow, serpentine movements.

One by one we slithered into the star-blown evening, proceeding single file, often crouching. I mimicked what I saw. I picked up on hand signals they communicated with and began to feel a deeper, nonverbal conversation taking place as well. We crawled into a field of crops. Intermixed with native-looking species of cactus and green and yellow brush were the remnants of corn plants. We stopped. I hadn't seen an actual corn plant since I was a kid, and rubbed an old piece of husk in my fingers. The vegetation flaked in my grip.

"It's decomposing, returning, so that the next crop can grow." Basil continued his whispered explanation. "Our friends taught us how to garden-farm in the desert. There's plots like this all over this land."

"Not like this right? Not corn—the blight in '09. Resistant seeds are like, more expensive than gold." That's what I thought, so I said it.

"These seeds <u>are</u> worth more than gold, but they ain't modified. Our friends, they've been saving 'em in their families for generations."

"Where are your 'friends' now?" I asked.

"Oh, they're around; we can't eat all the yield, but…we can't sell any, either. Too much heat from the Agri Agency.

I scanned the perimeter. We weren't alone. A cloaked mysterious individual was squatting not twenty feet from us, watching in silence. The bus ride, the conversations, all popped back into my head. The stars twinkled, and the breeze made me feel a thousand years old, and immortal. I could be myself with Basil and his band of right-living, ex-System folk.

So, again, I spoke. "Skin Walkers?"

Sand was ground into finer sand the instant my thought became audible. The slow twisting feet of several listeners put an end to my comfort zone. I could hear the land breathing, and the coyote crying from far away.

All eyes, seen and unseen, were on me now. I had said what the Indian man had told me not to say. Maybe out there, in the world where you cannot remember your morning, it was alright to forget such warnings. Out here, there was a contract, and the goose bumps on my flesh were telling me that breaking it has real consequences.

My brother was smiling, entertained, I realized, by the look of seriousness I wore.

"Yeah Gus, Skin Walkers."

Rita and Tara were respectfully giggling. A Viking-looking guy to whom I hadn't paid much attention until now held a raised thumb and nodded his approval, as well. I said what was on my mind, and it was still all right. I scanned the perimeter again, perhaps hoping to be given the nod of agreement by the unknown person who was watching us. It didn't happen.

I looked away and into the night's landscape, and although I felt ten thousand other eyes watching me, the night was all I could see.

*　　*　　*　　*

I ended up sleeping in a yurt. We lay out in a circle, a sort of octagon of males. It was fun. I heard about harvesting crops in the desert and about protecting the ranchers' cattle from a new species of coyote. What I knew about this place was all very fascinating, yet somehow I couldn't help feeling that I was hearing only the periphery of what life is like off the grid and out of the System. As much as I wanted to know about them, they seemed more eager to find out about me, what kind of a person I was. Basil had had some sort of life changing effect on them, and they looked for that same goodness in me. I could only give them what I was, and that night I was someone so tired and relieved to be rid of insomnia that I passed out in the middle of someone's story about a fantastic concert and a magical set that lasted all night long.

I slept hard. In the cocoon of a sleeping bag, I traveled far and wide. The great mystery of this massive expanse my mind explored satiated me in a holy and personal way. I could have stayed adrift through another night. I was awoken by Basil's playful push. I felt energized when I saw him. I was fully in the present, and awfully hungry. If I had to get up and leave the bliss of that puffy bag, I was hoping it was to move toward something edible. Basil assured me I would not be let down by Lulu's breakfast.

After we filled up the tank of the truck with homemade bio-diesel, we would be on our way. The unbelievably worked-on vehicle was literally held together by cables and ropes. It had formidable-looking tires and could carry more dusty travelers than its electric contemporaries. Basil knew when to slow down and speed up to power over great fissures in the road. On the straightaways he punched it, and with just me and him for passenger weight I tried not to entertain morbid thoughts of twisted metal and ironic family-reunion deaths.

Off the dirt road and onto the highway, the scenery changed. Occasional fields of green, and flocks of black and white sheep gave everything a toy train-set appearance. Ghostbead was coming up. As we banked around a corner, the entire town could be taken in at a glance. A church, white and wooden, was the area's skyscraper. A grocery store, farm supply shop, a restaurant, one motel, two gas stations and a bank made up the town's industry.

Apparently the Post Office pick-up was Basil's monthly ritual. All the community's members counted on him for packages, letters, and printed e-mails. Before we arrived, Basil gave me a bit of info on the demographic we were in. I already knew from my first night in town that this place was different; it had been clear then that I wasn't in New Jersey anymore.

According to Basil, townspeople's opinions of him were mixed. Many looked at the self-sufficient Warren as something peculiar, but good. Unfortunately, there were also individuals who chose to judge and look down upon the Warren as "recruitment dodgers" and even " pagans" and "black magic witches."

When we pushed the Post Office's door open, Sergeant Omni's look of displeasure met us. He held an apparently disappointing letter in his hand, and when he turned fast to look at us, a soft mechanical whine came from his neck area. He winced in pain as his one eye took us in.

Basil was practically underneath the shadow of Omni's chin when they both froze, then stared up and down at each other. My brother looked past Omni's mountainous chest, and instead of posturing himself, Basil became smaller and compassion welled in his eyes. "Whenever you're ready..."

Basil spoke to the large man's true self that had been locked somewhere inside of all the muscle and metal and pain of being a man alive in this swirling world of broken misconceptions.

Surprisingly, Omni finished Basil's sentence with, "I'm always welcome."

Basil smiled and said, "That's right brother," followed by a trusting, forearm gripping shake. "Always!"

The two locked arms and half hugged and I gave them room.

Basil then said, "She's making the right choices, Sarge; she's got the skills too, so don't worry."

This was about Omni's daughter. She'd gone down a self-destructive path as a teenager. The hero of foreign wars could not save the little girl whom he cared for more than anything else. Basil guided her, and the Warren put her on the path to help herself.

"She got stopped at the border." He explained his kid's situation to Basil like talking to a commander in a debriefing.

"She make it through?" When Basil asked that, I looked over my shoulder to see if anyone was following us.

"Yeah, 'course she did. That keed can con a cai-ote out of its skeen."

"Damn right she can. And has!"

They laughed together, and everything became lighter. I was proud of my brother.

Omni pocketed the letter and turned his eye toward me. I received respect by association and didn't really mind. Things could be worse. I nodded, and as he was leaving, told him, "I'll see you later."

Omni turned back at the door. "I knew you were kin...it's in the eyes."

$$* \qquad * \qquad * \qquad *$$

Basil pecked at the public access terminal. As he plugged in his information, the lady behind the counter said, "Mornin' Baze, y'all got a coupla packages."

Basil focused on the screen as if it was a painful task to be done quickly, and replied, "Oh, thanks, Meg, my brother—oh, Meg, this is my brother Gus. He'll go ahead and take 'em."

I thanked her as I filled the laundry bag Basil handed me.

Basil collected several printouts. He passed Meg a small green bundle from his shirt pocket and told her it would help her rheumatism. I shouldered the stuffed sack and joked that I felt like Santa Claus. Another dusty pickup truck slowed down in the road. Its time-etched driver just wanted to say 'hi' to Basil.

*　　　*　　　*　　　*

I used the last of my tip money to treat us both to omelets and pancakes. While waiting for Cowboy-Kid and the food to arrive, we had coffee and got to read some of the booty. Basil started on the e-mails. His brow furrowed in deep thought and he looked for his pipe to chew.

"What is it Basil?" The paranoia of a runaway was in my voice. "Something to do with me?"

He read, and located his pipe on the table.

I dropped down to a whisper. "Is it about…Skin Walkers."

"Yes, Gus." The wet pipe went into his pocket. "Actually that's exactly what it has to do with."

In the safety of the early morning, in that private space of a corner table, my brother weaved an incredible story. The Warren was a tale fit only for the ears of a few.

*　　　*　　　*　　　*

Lulu came with the steaming grub. The flapjacks hung over the sides of the dinner plates they were served on. I thought that the food would help me to cleanse my mind's palette.

Slurping at his steaming cup, Basil told me, "Hope you're well rested, it's gonna be a long night." I looked up with a generous syrupy portion in my mouth. Before I could ask a question Basil instructed me to, "Keep eating, Gussy. Eat, eat."

He reminded me of our mother at that moment—always serving and making sure everybody else was fed.

"When you're done, Gus, this one's for you." He handed me an envelope and a wrapped cigar box.

I drained my cup in hopes of diluting the mounds of hot cakes, eggs, and bacon now in my belly. Taking the mail addressed to me, I noticed that it had no return address. It was a greeting card with a big **Congratulations!** on the front. This was a cover, Alexander's attempt at subterfuge. Handwriting was scribbled across the card. The letter had an introduction that made me take heed of everything to follow:

Gus, burn this as soon as you are done reading it. Open the package only in privacy.

I am sending this to Basil's P.O. box in hopes that my private eyes were right about your location at the commune (or whatever he's calling it these days).

The syndicate who sent the assassin has been routed and eliminated. The attack on my house was what it took to get the Secular Army investigators involved.

You are in the clear; my cameras caught everything.

We're all being watched now.

The things I sent you are insurance.

You might not need to hear this right now, but things have changed for Demetrios. The United Free Balkans went under siege two days ago. He's been wounded. I made sure he received the best bionics surgery possible. He is in an induced cryogenic coma and rests in a restoration tank. He is alive. He will recover.

Gus, we can handle anything together. Be well, be smart, stay away from home for a while.

Give the family's love to Basil, we will give yours to Demetrios.

Please destroy this letter,

Your brother,

Alexander

✳   ✳   ✳   ✳

After passing on the information from Alex's card, I took a book of matches from the counter and burned it, as instructed, on the front steps of the café. My shock and worry from what I had read temporarily dissipated into the air with the smoke.

Cowboy-Kid followed us back to the Warren. The Kid buzzed with jumpy excitement. I held the wrapped cigar box on my lap. The moon was full, and tonight we were celebrating good things to come.

CHAPTER 12

▼

THE NARROW ROAD TO THE DEEP NORTH

Purity is water
translucent yet pregnant
with substance.
There is purity in words
when you wait for them to come.
People are pure
during fearless moments
exchanging poetry
under distant stars.

The scent of burning tamarisk filled the barn. The Middle Eastern tree grew well in this desert, and smelled like a Greek church when added to the fire. Fritz strummed on his acoustic. He wore small, wire-rimmed spectacles. The thick lenses made his bright blue eyes appear enormous. The instrument caused him to hunch over. Knotted dirty-blonde hair jutted from his head like a dusty lion's mane. He appeared spacey to me, distant but happy.

The musician had met my brother in APTR Care almost a decade ago. Basil was a councilor with Ancient Passages to Recovery when Fritz was delivered from a Canadian psych ward.

Now he played and sang as I sipped from a warm jelly jar. I watched and listened:

*"Well, the first days are the hardest days
don't you worry anymore"*

He had told me how it was his first time, how Synth was going around his scene and he wanted it to sharpen his musician's ear. He did too much and the batch was too strong.

*"When life looks like Easy Street
there is danger at your door"*

Fritz had really lost his shit. He'd spent two weeks drifting before ending up in an Iowa shelter.

*"Think this through with me
let me know your mind"*

His partner, Annie, was as woodsy and cherubic as he was. Basil held a special affinity for these two.

*"Wo-oah, what I want to know
is are you kind?"*

He played on while Basil piled envelopes and packages in the middle of the room. Fritz and Annie soon switched to a rhythmic double drumming. More people arrived and formed a circle around the things that had traveled in from the outside world.

Many humbly discovered the new possessions that they would not keep for themselves. After examining a blanket, or knife, or book, they each made a special gesture toward another resident. Each person seemed to give away his or her new-found item with a smile and hug.

I was given a field-guide for edible plants from the Viking. I offered him a wrinkled paperback that I retrieved from my gym-bag. He accepted it joyfully and told me, "I have never read Basho, but it will comfort me during the growing season."

The two players loyally kept a beat. They were so consistent in their job that they seemed to disappear and leave the sound of drums as their only footprint. The Viking picked up a large, straight stick and began to back up the duet by thudding the butt of his lance against the floor boards. Someone they called Finder joined in on the same beat. He had earned this nickname while working with Basil in APTR Care. Finder could track runaway patients quickly and often in the dark of night. He held the lance with both hands and looked almost comical when he stood next to the much taller and more composed Norseman.

Rita showed up and entered the now clear center circle right away. She moved her limbs in a way that became more animallike with each thump of the drum. Her gait was that of a cat. Just then Muso crept out from behind a tapestry. A wave of relief flooded my perception as the orange feline climbed into his old clothing-filled home.

I allowed myself to be mesmerized by the female panther, who was my brother's mate. A howl rang out and triggered a cacophony of calls and natural songs.

"Woooooooooooo...woooooooooooooooo!"

Everybody moved in the same direction. Many moved low to ground. Basil's arms extended behind him and became wings. He soared with a piercing "Kaawww!"

I stepped forward and slipped slightly on the sweat of seventeen shifting human shapes. Even Cowboy-Kid looked like he was in another world. He slithered on the ground and raised his torso like a sniffing snake clad in denim. Nobody judged, everybody was in.

My foot slipped again and recovered itself by becoming a bear paw. I pace-walked by moving one side of my body at a time. Great strength surged through my body. I snorted and smelled the air. Everyone carried a different scent. Several in the party appeared to take on more than one new identity. Even their odor somehow seemed to shift with every new gait or posture.

Cowboy-Kid moved to the door and lit up a cigarette to watch the sun disappear. He used the tobacco to purposely bring himself back to the two-legged world. His keys jingled when it was time for him to go.

*   *   *   *

Hours passed, and after several second-winds our cups got filled with water and cold tea. The drumming slowed, and dancers dispersed throughout the barn on light feet. They picked up shoulder bags and small packs. They tied back long hair and patted their flushed faces. Many bodies gave off steam, and the floor held slippery puddles. Basil gave me a nod from across the room. The intensity in his eyes made me feel that something serious was about to happen. I suddenly wanted to be near Basil, and when I approached we were respectfully given space by the others.

My brother handed me a packed canvas bag and bedroll to crisscross against my body. He checked me before leading the community into the tunnel. The cool earth refreshed everybody's hot skin. As if we pushed through a giant living being, rebirth was sure to happen when we entered the naturally well-lit night.

In single file and practically in each other's footprints, the Warren ran effortlessly to an inaudible beat. We entered a new meditation of movement. An invisible string seemed to connect us. I felt a pull from my center point. My *dan-tien* guided me, my body followed. Polaris indicated that our direction was west.

The moccasins let me feel the ground. I was amazed to be unconsciously hopping over cactus, and ducking under crooked tree branches. Hours went by and still we ran. Every chapter of my life played out in my head, back-dropped by the eternal star-speckled blanket.

We ran, and ran, and ran, until I thought the sun began to glimmer on our sweat soaked backs. We arrived at Dripping Rock and sipped from the cool waters that oozed cleanly from a giant and ancient stone. Humans had sipped from the site for centuries. It was the waterhole of coyotes and shape-shifters.

Basil quenched himself and stood with a dripping head before howling out a beautiful and eerie cry, "Woooooo…Wooooo…Woooooo…"

He was answered back from a high-up cave.

"Woooooo…Wooooo…Woooooo…"

Our group stopped drinking and followed Basil's quiet and stealthy climb. We reached a cave that could not be seen from the waterhole. The narrow mouth we entered required us to crouch and crawl. The interior of the cave was black as pitch. No one stood—for fear of meeting a rock ceiling with his or her skull. Strong, shadowy bodies already occupied the space and were only seen in glimpses of flickering reflected light. The Warren folk crawled in to join the large circle. Everyone was silent. After a time all breathing seemed to synchronize.

Glowing orbs floated into view, settling in the center. I reckoned the orange objects to be hot rocks, and that this dark, natural room was to become a stony sweat lodge. The air became increasingly hot as broken antlers carried in more and more glowing stones. Steam filled my nostrils and caused my nose to run with mucous. My body's own water bathed me, and I sat in a salty puddle of my own perspiration. The water hissed on the hot rocks, producing an invisible cloud of sage-smelling steam. *"Hissss!"*

A hoarse but youthful voice then broke the humid silence.

"I carry the ladle tonight. In this first round, I would like to pray for our brothers and sisters who suffer, those injured, the invisible people, street folk, the locked-up, junkies, those sick with diseases, those sick with war, the poor in spirit from all over the earth. In this first round I would like to pray for them."

Several voices, beginning to exhibit the fatigue of extreme heat, responded with the word:

"Support."

"Support."

"Support."

No matter how hard I strained my eyes to see, only a curtain of blackness greeted my gaze. I stopped trying, and meditated on the gruff voice's words. Serge and Nekros and both Tadas had all been killed. I pictured their faces and thought peaceful things, for they were people whose lives were surrounded in violence.

My mind traveled to the old hospital room. The fear of dying and becoming a statistic on a doctor's clipboard overwhelmed me. I saw the bed that I had lain in for fourteen days. With my mind's eye I stared at the patient. To my horror, as the bedridden man rolled over, I saw Demetrios, my brother, unconscious and heavily bandaged.

I heard myself whimper out a denial, "No...." My teary words got louder, "Please, he does not deserve this, take my life and make him better."

The ladle-pourer responded, and "Support" whispered through the steam.

I left the hospital to let my brother sleep. New York City and all the people that the hustle passes over enveloped my mental sight. William Ringle and his mature kindness walked the streets, was ignored by Suits who probably could not even hold a proper and educated conversation with him. I felt my own teeth clench and upper lip tremble. Martha sat alone in my hospital room. Wyeth stared into the television. My parents walked their quiet house and lit candles for their missing children. All the faces, the soft eyes that were or are children, cried alone.

Whimpering. Sobbing. Someone next to me gave up their water. Someone across from me let go of their emotions and they trickled out in soft, steady prayers. I became freer in the darkness. Like a great geyser bursting, I let tears roll over my cheeks and into my mouth. My prayers had the flavor of my pain. It felt good, to not be thinking of just my own survival, but of the well-being of others. The millions, billions, the unseen, were my family, and it hurt to know that even one person would pass through this world, through some city or shelter, jail or concrete jungle, unknown and untouched by the kindness of another human. I internalized the suffering, shaking, and dying, and poured them back out digested by my awareness of them.

My tears flowed, and I tried to capture the image of every invisible person that I saw only in my periphery. I prayed to…to God, the greatest good, who must have heard my sincerity. I had never prayed like that before and I felt light. I let go, and gave myself up to my creator. I felt powerless in the shadow of the world's sadness, and liberated by my own meekness.

Hisss! Water hit the hot rocks and a billow of steam reheated me and carried me farther and farther into the purity of prayer.

The voice spoke again:

"Our planet suffers. I will pray for the health of our birth mother."

I spoke, "The earth is suffering as well…the macro becomes the micro. Suffering has increased on every level, from space garbage scraping over the orb skin of our atmosphere down to the cancer cells which encircle healthy life. We know the summer comes by looking at the trees. We know it is near, look at the planet. Burning sphere, poisoned water, miracles made extinct. Who else could be its governor? The devil plots to ruin God's green earth."

My hands gripped the mud beneath my legs, and when swiped onto my shoulders, cooled my skin. Through dirt smeared lips I mumbled, "Bless this place, this living thing we are made of."

"Support, Support, Support."

Someone proclaimed "Door!" Almost instantaneously a breeze moved through the cave; it was accompanied by moonlight. More rocks came in, large and glowing, pregnant with energy. Someone crawled out. The chamber resealed. Darkness, darker than before, settled like a cartoonist's black ink around the edges of a scene.

Hisss!

"In this last round I will pray for our enemies. For those who wish us harm. In this round, I'll pray for them." The ladle pourer had spoken.

People were lying down and melting. Quarts of water were coming out through transpiration. There was nowhere for the moisture to go. Condensation collected. It rained in the darkness. With every hot inhalation my mind came closer and closer to resting. My spirit stretched forth and smiled.

I might have just mouthed the words. I could have been thinking them. Without bodily sensations to notify me it didn't much matter. "My enemies…those who wish me harm. The Sensei. I'll pray for him."

I was over-thinking. Just then I returned to the flesh. My very real ears were picking up a voice from outside of the lodge.

"My student…pupil Con-stan-tine. Why do you pray for me? Come to me now. Sit here and talk."

It was the Sensei. Pasito's voice was more snakelike then I had remembered. In the heat of the ancient sauna a cold chill trickled down my spine. My fear built up like the drip-filled puddles in the lodge.

The fierce specter called me from outside of the cave and made my dark sanctuary into a confining space where I felt powerless, without control and utterly naked. As the eerie words repeated themselves over and over inside my head, my expression of fear came out suddenly and in a single word, "Door!"

I had already begun moving when the stone barrier was rolled away and the chill of night crept inside. My pulse quickened and my knees pressed into the sand. As I went out from the warm, moist shelter, steam rose from my slick skin. The seal was put back, and moonlit earth greeted my eager eyes. My sight did not provide release from fear, but instead multiplied it. From the shadow of an old and twisted juniper stepped forth the ghost of the dojo. He looked almost regal in a flowing robe. Standing next to a natural bonsai tree, he wore the sword that I once held in meditation.

He gestured for me to sit. Wary from fear, shivering from cold, I approached the long-dead master. The closer I got to him, the warmer he became. Finally, I knelt at an arm's length, and relaxed in the ghost's temperate aura. Pasito elevated his scabbard so as not to scrape the ground with it. He knelt, eye to eye with me.

"I am not flattered by your prayers. I am saddened by your poor choices. You pray to some God for the benefit of enemies, and make me the object of your conscience-cleansing. Me, who has given you so much."

My thighs began to shake, and the pebbles beneath my bare shins pressed in and prodded me to stand and then run. But I did not. I breathed, as deeply as I could. I met the strange image before me with courage.

"You…torment…me…you are a dark spirit."

"A dark spirit who has shown you the martial way! You should be praying for the ones who took away your birthright. The ones who tried to lump you in with the rest of the herd so that you would never assume your true destiny. The ones who will tremble in fear when you do step forward. The ones who hate you for not being a simpleton, a commoner, and a slave."

"Please let me be," I pleaded.

The spirit continued his tirade, unabated by my rejection, feeding on my fears. "Your talent has been wasted because of fools and bullies, the unexamined, the sheep, who have pressed their dull faces against your backside and softly and cowardly nudged you out of your place in the world. You are conscious, and that is why you have suffered so. You have yet to reap the reward of your pain! If it is up to the envious ones who cast the illusion of control, then you never will be who you really are!

"Go to the cliff's edge, my sleeping king, and take your physical life. Do this and be the cutter of ignorance! Be the slayer of drunken leadership that is bent on driving Utopia to ruin. I beseech you to join the warmth of the world that the minions cannot see. "All the Tadas in the world cannot hurt you. Why? Because you are awakened, O Warrior-Buddha. Now apply but an ounce of your strength to the scales of truth, and balance this world with the suffering of your enemies."

I breathed in, but felt myself weakening. This creature before me glowed with hatred. I thought of how much warmer my scared and naked self could become if I, too, surrendered to the hatred that squirmed for room inside of my own reptilian brain. Then, from the hidden fire that warmed the sweat-lodge's rocks, came the odor of faith. Truth rose in the smoke of burning tamarisk. The smell of true power enlivened something inside my heart.

"Leave...me...alone," I implored.

He responded to my protest, "I have given you the Mountain Storm, yet still you run, and hide in a hole with...animal people."

"I am my own governor," was my continued defiance.

He kept up the attack. "I entrusted you with the knowledge of my master who, as we speak, patiently awaits your arrival."

I blurted, "I defeated your man!"

He kept on. "Because of the *Kuji-Kiri* knowledge you can defeat many foes!"

"I have my free will."

"What angers me most of all is that you turn from the gift of immortality."

Another voice joined the mix, "Put him behind you, Gus!" It was Basil, from atop the sweat-lodge.

Basil went on, "Your will is stronger than all the temptations!"

Rita was with him. She stood straight and naked, glistening like boggy water at first light.

I held my eyes on the Sensei as I prepared to deliver a final response. "You offered me slavery, and the death of my true soul." I clasped my palms and interlocked my fingers in the sign for protection against harm. "I reject your offer of this dark gift. With a clear and unpolluted mind, I choose to walk my own path."

The smile flashed. He did a barely noticeable bow. With a single step into a shadow, the spirit was gone.

*　　*　　*　　*

We climbed down into the clean waters. We drank, washed, and recovered our clothing. The three of us walked together to one of the concealed fires. Tara was already there, staring into the small dancing flames. She looked at peace with the moment. The corner of a rock monolith provided cover and reflected the flame's heat onto our replenished skin. I had greater clarity of all my senses. Never have I exhaled and inhaled so well. We made tea and stoked the fire for the others who would be finishing their own battles, epiphanies, healings and births.

*　　*　　*　　*

As our fire became smaller, a canine communication could be heard; it sounded as if its talkers were approaching. When pulsing orange coals outnumbered flames, a distant movement caught my eye. I did not tell the others.

Relief came to me when someone spoke. Tara asked a question that only a trusted stranger could ask, "So what's the answer?"

"The answer?" I asked back.

"Yeah, the answer for you. The one you came out here for."

I thoughtfully exhaled and tried to let my response just come. "Well, my destiny, its…up to me. How I choose to live, how I choose to think."

"And how is that, Gus?"

"I don't know."

"Know what?"

"How I choose to live or think."

"What do you know?"

"How I will choose not to live."

"Sounds like freedom."

"Isn't real freedom spiritual? Isn't the world enslaved by death?" I was happy with the clarity of my words. I wasn't sure if my thoughts were too morbid for someone so earthy.

"Sounds pretty heavy," she correctly observed.

"I guess."

She eased up. "I respect you. You're very sincere."

I was flattered, but too drained to blush. Tara became the most beautiful and ancient piece of landscape at that moment.

So as not to become inebriated by the pleasantness of the moment and say something I might come to regret, I moved my awareness away from her. I looked far into the night. A bear appeared to be crawling on its belly, approaching our conversation! To my even greater surprise, the stalking animal stood up on two legs!

A man wearing the coat of a black bear stood motionless, staring toward our glowing space. The snout pointed upward, and I watched him tilt back further and expel a throaty howl. *"Oooooooohh!"* The cry echoed off the sandstone cliffs and the ground became enlivened.

A woman stood up from near the feet of the one howling. Rocks unfolded, trees stepped into motion. Then the sand itself released a troupe of shape-shifters!

I instinctively backed up. Basil's hand came to rest on my shoulder and he assured me, "It's all right, he's the Voice from our Sweat. We call him Oso, the Bear."

*   *   *   *

I quietly ate oatmeal and jerky. I was immersed in a humble enjoyment of my wide-open senses. Oso ate with his back to the fire and wore sunglasses over his eyes. A musky odor wafted over from the fur-clad figure. Metal cups and small cans got filled with hot chocolate.

I put my empty dinnerware on the sand and found my small pack. I filled my hands with the cigars Alex sent me. Oso smiled appreciatively. We all smoked, and listened to the desert sing.

After a long while I walked away from the firelight. A green wool blanket kept me warm. I observed the moon illuminating a distant earthen range. Snow reflected the blue light atop Sleeping Buffalo. The mountain deserved this name for it seemed to be resting on four buckled legs and a mighty collapsed head. The distant figure appeared peaceful in sleep.

*   *   *   *

Before my exhausted body could nod off completely by the fire, two people dreamily showed me to a sleeping area. The night of dancing, running and sweating had wiped me out. I had met new people and experienced profound things, but the need for sleep made the surreal simply acceptable. Beneath a rocky overhang was dug what resembled a shallow grave. A mattress of yellow cottonwood leaves lined the pit. Mounds of dirt lay loosely piled. I was so tired that I unquestioningly lay down. Still wrapped in wool, I allowed myself to be buried. A breathable cloth covered my face. My mouth and nose remained exposed for air.

The soil was heavier than I expected. At first my chest heaved in sudden panic. I remembered childhood vacations at the beach and playing in the ocean's sand. My memories comforted me. I looked forward to an uninterrupted rest within the cozy cocoon of earth.

*   *   *   *

The sun rose, and still I slept as if my body were dead. When at last I woke the dew drops were drying. A corked gourd filled with water and minty leaves lay near my head. I cracked through my soil shell and drank generously. After a stretch and a steamy piss, I meandered quietly around the site. I hoped to find some morning company, and maybe even some cocoa. I stepped lightly over cactus flowers and crypto-biotic soil. I was careful not to wake the ground.

Everything appeared so different in the morning. The night was immediate and whatever was in my personal space became the world. The evening was also about experiencing the great distance of stars. The far off night sky allowed for a feeling of comfortable smallness. Beneath the cover of darkness things greater than myself were at work.

This morning's light had exposed a country of small hills. Everywhere I looked there were mounds of rock and earth that blocked easy navigation. I knew these were the terrestrial waves that did not appear on contour maps. They were high enough to hinder travel, but short enough to be excluded from identification because they were not quite forty feet tall. A stranger to this land might be caused some discomfort in travel by these anonymous obstacles. I was still emotionally drained from yesterday's accomplishments. I wasn't awake enough to worry.

Where was the fire? I wondered. Surely our supper area could not have melted like frost with the coming of sunlight. I decided to make my bed by filling it in with dirt. I would then shoulder my canteen and blanket and see if I couldn't find at least the smell of their breakfast fire. A crow, large and carbon-black, perched on the closest hill. I took the bird's landing as a sign to change my vantage point.

Chalky rock gave way and crumbled with each step up the mound. I slid and jabbed my fingers into the hillside for balance. Once at the top, perspiration beaded on my forehead and salty water dripped into my lips. The crow had flown, and I searched the terrain for him with my eyes. Remarkably, the land returned images devoid of people.

Shit! Did I walk away from them? I should have stayed put near my bed. I'll just go back, back to the overhang I slept under, and wait for them to wake up.

I slid down in a zigzag pattern. Dust kicked up during my descent. The bed area had disappeared. To my growing horror, nothing looked familiar. The sun was nearly above me and sent down rays that made my head very hot. I looked around for the highest hill again. I saw what I thought was the best watchtower and sprinted up it. Finally at the top, I breathed heavily and struggled to recall familiar landmarks.

The gathering was held within a rocky corner. I thought I spied the crevice, it was just over two more small hills and past a dried up creek. Then I saw relief. In the distance, someone was standing, back turned and wearing a pointed, round sun hat. The person was in the very spot where we had gathered. Wasting no time, I bolted down. Soon my pace changed to a fast walk. I almost turned an ankle and did spill some water. I let out a loud "I'm coming!" to the waiting friend.

Stepping into the dehydrated creek bed brought more relief. I had seen that someone was standing and waiting, probably for me, just on the other side. I guessed that this person thought that he was the first to awaken and was respectfully awaiting the breakfast call.

Busted-up dry tree limbs were thrown about, as was the scattered skeleton of a cow. The way out of the creek was almost ninety degrees up. With the help of exposed tree roots, I knew I could climb up with a little effort. Almost able to peek over the rim, hoping my sun hat wearing friend was still there, I suddenly became filled with a primal fear and wonder.

A great noise coupled with a strong vibration had frozen me. Both elbows were just over the side when the quake climaxed and stopped. I pulled up and knelt on the bank when I saw the beast that could literally shake the earth. Its black eye was the size of my own fist. It smelled the air which probably reeked with my scent. Its nostrils snorted and its feet did a little stutter step. A dozen or so other bison had just put the brakes on behind this leader, who found it necessary to deal with me in some way. The desert was an ocean, and I felt meek without a boat.

I'm dead, I thought. *There is nothing I can do to prevent this creature from running me through if he chooses to do so. When he's done, his troupe can use me for a foot mat. Maybe these guys met the owner of those cow bones. Trampled and left to decompose in the hot sun.*

The alpha animal just breathed. It was becoming for me a moment somehow outside of time. It was happening, but was also like a dream.

This is it. No where to hide. It doesn't hate me, I know that, and if I die right now, it will be okay because of this moment. Did I want to go out scared and cold and timid? Did I want to die full of hatred for my killer? No! In fact, in fact I felt love for this…this great living churner of earth.

His massive horned head, capable of plowing through five-foot walls of snow with ease, began to drop. I simply and slowly touched my palms together in a prayerful posture. I bowed my head and put forth love. It was my death decision and it was righteous.

I felt tremors and rocky soil bombard my knees, and dust cloud around my face. I remained in this position for a long time. Quiet came. I don't know how long I was there, but when I stood, still intact, I headed toward the green hat in the distance.

I held on to the image of the magnificent buffalo. My heart still jumped when a rabbit burst from a nearby bush. It leaped, then skidded to somewhere safe. A fine gray powder dappled the ground from where the animal burst. The ash revealed its footprints.

My goal, the broad green hat, was like one that might be worn by a farmer in China. I recognized, however, that it was woven from the yucca leaves of this wilderness. The body it rested on was not what I had hoped. The motionless model was actually a tall walking stick. The dinner fire was gone. Not an ember remained.

*   *   *   *

The hat fit my head comfortably. It even had a chinstrap of soft leather. The staff that had been speared into the ground felt good in my hand. I enjoyed moving the stick through the air as Serge had trained me to do in The Gym. I stood there for a time, staring off into the distance. The great visor shielded me from the sun. The sun had seemed to do much more traveling at that point than I had done during the day. She was dipping toward the horizon. I wrapped the blanket around me and sat with crossed legs. I drained the rest of my cool drink and let the staff rest across my lap. I was happy to be alive. I hadn't been trampled to death by a fear of nature. The scarecrow was a gift and had assured me that someone was around and looking out for me. I smiled in the shade of the big hat and daydreamed. My stomach growled and my imaginings soon turned to fantasy.

*   *   *   *

A body can last three weeks without food. If a person is not used to fasting however, a single day without eating can prove extremely challenging. Without my journal to scribble in I whispered to myself.

I don't have my poems with me now. If I did then I would revel in their companionship and pour over their pages like a master chef over a fine cut, careful with my spices, gentle with tenderizing, but in complete enjoyment of the task at hand, and always ready to revise with extra oils and snippets of garlic. Hunger is the best appetizer. A steak, salad first of course. Then a large bowl of chowder. A spring water with a lime, or even a clear soda to drink. The steak must be large and cooked medium— well with an equally large baked potato smothered in sour cream. Perhaps a vegetable like buttered asparagus. The salad's dressing is oil and vinegar and the soup is served with crackers. Desert. Desert is chocolate cheesecake with whipped cream. Coffee to wash it down—two cups, perhaps even three. In between the second and third cup I am allowed a cigarette. The old kind with regular straight-up tobacco. The steak has onions in small amounts and a special spicy sauce at the ready if needed. After dinner I can take a hot shower, but not before I pour a bourbon with ice and ginger ale while waiting for my date to arrive. When she does rap on the door I am clean and offer her a drink. Soon I can take a full-bellied nap and have a smoke with a huge smile on my face. I can do yoga to relax my eating muscles. Before I know it its time for breakfast. While the coffee is brewing I sip a salty Bloody Mary and crack eggs for an omelet. My date makes the toast while I go to work mixing in feta cheese that has a bite. I slice ice-cold tomatoes. We feast and drink the coffee. Quiet time comes where I can write poems, snack on chocolate-covered almonds, and read through some translations of Buddhist sutras. After time for digestion I work off breakfast with a jog. We catch an early movie. And next thing we know it's on to dinner!

*   *   *   *

My food fantasy was entertaining, but when it ended I was even hungrier. I sucked on little cloud-blue juniper berries. The wooden marbles made my saliva became pasty. My body soon became cold. I curled up in the shelter I had dug. Soft tree parts, leaves, grasses, and rubber rabbitbrush surrounded me.

My burial wasn't meticulous. Raindrops awakened me. My cheeks were being pelted by water. I curled into a fetal position, like a flea in the sand. The blanket inched its way over my face. Too tired to rise, I hoped my hat would catch this rain in its bucket. Sleep did not come as it did the night before. My attempt at rest was fitful, and dreams mingled with waking reality. I was buried alive and shaking. Cold liquid crept around my backside. A pool gathered around my spine. Too exhausted to move, my body's heat flickered like the rocks in the sweat lodge, and resiliently struggled to stay alive.

$$* \qquad * \qquad * \qquad *$$

Morning brought birds and cacophonic melodies. The rain let up, and to my joy was brimming over inside my head-gear. My bones felt as if they would crack like glass rods as I stood. Shakily, but with great attention, I filled my gourd. After drinking, I attempted a stretch and watched the world come alive with the rising sun.

Wrapped in wet wool, I secured my hat, shouldered the canteen, and stepped out with stick in hand. The dawn could be better enjoyed from a high perch. I climbed a gray hill slowly. I wasn't going to let myself become winded or even damper with sweat. Each break on the way up was a chance to let the sun dry me, and a moment of inspiration. I quenched my thirst and drained the canteen before coming to rest atop the hill.

I remember saying aloud,

"I sit here on this high mound, and am awed by it all. Sun is climbing, or retreating. Dawn, or twilight, is upon us. The mountains are red and still, yet they move. Should I watch this ant climb toward me? The hills pull my gaze in opposite directions, demanding I look at the panorama, prodding me to enter a higher brain function. This is not how the majority experiences the world. I sit and am small and big at the same time. I will stay here, in this great place, and pray for real things, and purpose outside of myself."

There was peace outside my body. When I lifted the empty drinking gourd the thought of time sadly came to me. How long had I been sitting and sweating in the heat of the sun's light? How long could I do without more water? My old consciousness was aroused. My brain spun with the pain of dehydration and hunger. Feet kicked inside the walls of my skull.

I fingered the ground for something smooth to press to my lips. A mollusk shell, spiral in shape and golden in design, brought me to a cracked smile. A shell; insignificant to the well-fed and easily-bored observer was ethereal in the hand of a spiritual being questing for cleansed perception. Lifting it to my mouth, I remembered my excesses and the part they played in getting me to this moment.

I was through with Synthetic Synergy, but could recall the good feeling of surrendering to the pattern around me. I kissed that shell and took in a galactic hit that turned up the volume in the orchestra of planets.

Nature is unstoppable. It is just a matter of time.

White rabbits appeared from holes in the ground. I watched as a fat bunny squirmed from a subterranean depth. Next to it another one surfaced. In the distance two popped up, and next to them a group of three climbed out. A scuffle from behind had me turning to watch five rabbits appear, then I counted eight from another hole, and stopped counting when thirteen scratched their way out from beneath the dirt floor. The desert had become carpeted with soft, living coats of white.

A shadow lurked among unstained carpet. A coyote was coming and was creeping through the endless field of rabbits. Panic was not in the air, nor was hunger. The canine looked like she was resting on several fluffy pillows and I closed my eyes to what I thought was an absurd vision. All was dark beneath her eyes.

I could see that my surroundings were different and that I was suddenly standing on scorched earth. As quick as a blink I had been moved to a new location that reeked of violence.

"Get down!", commanded a voice. "The sun's almost set and they'll be comin'."

Obeying the voice I climbed down into a trench. It was dark and the men I saw were dirty, armed, and clearly buzzing with alertness.

"What is this place?" I asked.

"What...? You with any reinforcements? Radio man is with Chief in the center of our perimeter. Didn't think he got through to anyone yet. Nips will be movin' on us any minute."

Thunder cracked and rain spit down.

"Great," said the young soldier who spoke with me. "What next?"

A whistle pierced through the pitter-patter and an explosion followed. *Boom!*

Smoke lifted from the center of what I reasoned was a dug-in fortification. I realized I was with a group of soldiers defending themselves against a Japanese attack force. My new friend and I peeked from our trench and were horrified at the sight of the dead and smoldering radio man and commanding officer.

"Fuck...let's go...ahh...?"

"Gus, my name is Gus."

"Okay. Gus, here's the skinny: our plan for getting help just got hit by a mortar. We got no leadership, either. Let's run the circle and see if anyone's got a clue."

We moved quickly, in darkness, within the dug-in fortification. Every twenty feet or so we met GIs who were all wondering the same thing: "What do we do now?"

By the time we made it back to the original hole, an eerie chant could be heard rising in the distance:

"Sayonara, Joe! Die, Joe! Fuck you, Joe!"

The sun had set, and in the grayness of dusk I felt a vague familiarity about the young American soldier.

"That's the usual thing," said my new buddy, "'Fuck Joe', that's all the English they know. Then...they move in on us."

I watched him check his M-1 rifle and get into firing position. He flashed me a smile before going back to squinting down the barrel.

I gasped in a realization.

"Most guys blow the water drop out of their sight and refocus," he said. "I don't. The water becomes a lens and I just adjust my fire. The Japs are tough, but they can't think for themselves. Without leadership they fall apart." He wore a somber face as he added, "That's why we shoot the best-dressed first."

The cursing and threats continued, "Sayonara, Joe!"

The rain was hitting hard.

"Die, Joe!"

I looked at my own water-slicked hands to keep from going mad.

"Fuck, Joe!"

Then the enemy's yells ceased.

The noisy downpour persisted, but I think I had gone deaf. The GIs were pointing muzzles in the direction of the evil screams.

A new battle cry rose from the silence. The unknown echoed with, "Banzai! Banzai! Banzai!"

"This is it, this is it, shoot well, gun, aim straight, eye, squeeze steady, finger."

"Banzai!"

Bang! Bang! Bang!

The Japs were charging with foot-long razors at the end of their rifles. The blades glistened in the darkness of the incoming terror.

"Banzai!"

Bang! Bang! Bang!

132   Naked Among the Tombs

Bodies fell, grenades exploded, dying men screamed, and steel tore into flesh. It was Pasito, and he was efficiently picking off the invaders. The American soldier was Pasito's past self, before he became the minion of Hachiman.

Bang! Bang! Bang!

Then finally it was over.

*   *   *   *

I sat with the marksman and listened with ringing ears as the storm came to a halt.

"Got a light?" he asked.

Medics were working, people gagging, hands trying to cover mortal wounds. The enemy's war cries were no more.

"Say, fella, got a light?" asked Pasito again.

"Sorry, no."

He put the cigarette behind his ear and held his head in his hands.

"Once you take out their leader, everything will fall apart," explained the young future Sensei.

The drained warrior turned to me with tear filled eyes. "Once you take a man's life, everything changes. You fall, and spend the rest of your days climbing out."

With that great truth imparted to me, the battle-worn soldier climbed out of the ditch and informed me, "I'm gonna find a light."

Stepping over a corpse he picked up a smoldering rag and lit his smoke. Exhaling, he looked to me once more. "Remember what I told you." Flashing a smile, he walked off.

*   *   *   *

When I opened my eyes the rabbits and their holes were no longer. Only a dusting of trackless snow remained. The coyote was sitting upright on a rock, legs crossed, and happily smoking a cig through a permanent smile. I closed my eyes and the image was gone.

Standing for a long time, a deep sense of wonder consumed me. I contemplated the meanings of apocalypse. At that moment I knew that the catastrophe had already happened a billion times over. It was, in fact, happening today.

The junky sitting in darkness and pain, young bellies filled with gas instead of food, land mines disguised as dolls; it is savagery, and inhumanity. Apocalypse is a bird arriving home after winter migration to land on a cold, gray cell phone tower, and not the embrace of a familiar tree. It happens to the average, to the iconic, and to the invisible. It may be you right now. The quest for immortality is a slavery and an empty trail sought by the misguided. Eternity is in the quest to connect with all life. Physical death is but a transfer of energy.

*   *   *   *

A song awakened me from a sweet rest. My lids fluttered open and I realized that I was splayed out on the mound of earth. The chanting was native but somehow familiar to me.

Others were coming, drawn in by the hymn. By the time the song ended a circle had formed. I didn't bother with trying to figure out how so many people materialized from the vacant desert. I just straightened my back and prepared for church.

An old man in a flannel shirt and two gray braids put his palm up in my direction and said, "Hi Gus, glad you could make it."

I nodded in thanks. I realized I lacked the necessary energy in my face to reply, or even to smile.

The large circle of people sat down. All eyes fell upon Oso.

"Blessed be brothers and sisters."

"Blessed be!" proclaimed the crowd.

"Many of us have walked in spirit these days, and while our bodies went hungry our real selves were nourished. I walked in dreams and saw many of your snowy visions. I tell you this day, my brothers and sisters, that the snow you saw is the North Country, and the time has come to leave the desert!"

I undid the strap and let my hat fall behind me.

"There is nothing to be sad about now, because with each challenge we grow stronger in spirit!"

"Support!" replied the captive audience.

"As we commune, my friends, remember that your vision is your own, and the North Country can be the Great Mountains. It can also be the cold temper of the outside world that many of us must return to."

He scanned the crowd with spotlight eyes and said, "Or perhaps see for the first time. The shape-shifter is holy and has much work to do. Now, receive nourishment with me and be strong in both worlds."

A basket of flat bread stood near Oso. He held in his hands a large leather flask which seemed ready to be poured. One by one, the circle moved toward him and received the bread and drank from the skin. While the soft march progressed the people sang different songs. They were songs that made my heart dance. I felt uplifted. Like when the yiayias sang, only different.

Before grasping the container my right thumb and first two fingers touched. The lesson of the *Kuji-Kiri* echoed in my head: when one reaches a certain level of training the hands automatically form the finger locks. I touched them to my forehead, then to my center, then my right shoulder, then left, and settled my open hand on my *dan-tien*. This was the sign of the cross that I had learned so long ago when I first stood in church and felt the rays of the sun warm me through stained glass.

I was thankful as I grasped the bread and drank of the liquid. I was thankful beyond words, and for the first time words, and thoughts that were based on words, drifted away and a letting-go took place. Thinking was not a proof of existence. Consciousness was something more mysterious. It was this mystery that the mind conspired against in all my days. The spirit of the Sensei was part of the mystery. The fearful thoughts of the past had twisted my perception of Pasito's true self.

This thing I found in the desert was freedom. It was surrendering to the greatest good. I walked in beauty and knew that art's true meaning is not to capture, but to conjoin with this unspeakable wonder and share it with all life. The giving of this good, which is love, is the very essence of the great mystery.

I ate of the bread and drank of the tea and looked up and around at the miracle that was existence. The sky parted in a great smile of joy. Rocks massaged the soles of my feet in play. Trees made music with the wind. The people around me in all their different colors and shapes and sizes were the greatest gifts of all. Heroic and majestic people. Each individual with a story. Each with a universe of love inside his or her heart. Life was an eternal dance and celebration and praise of the creator of all things, who moved through all things, and was here right now where simple folks gathered.

*   *   *   *

For three weeks more we would live together in the desert. Basil returned the shoulder bag. He called it my Possible Sack. It contained everything I'd possibly need to survive. I undid the canvas ties and curiously examined the bag for the first time, like a child in a Christmas stocking. After learning about the shelter materials, water purifiers and gatherers, fire tools, food rations and small game traps I decided to have a cigar.

The box was still half full of stogies. I held one firmly in my teeth as I searched the box. I discovered two stacks of Banco bills wrapped in a white silk handkerchief. The international currency was all powerful and I was shocked to be holding the blue bills in my sun-browned hands.

The silk continued to unravel like a magician's prop and uncovered something that astonished me even more than the loot.

The rectangular item I found was heavy in my hand. The discovery was the size of a deck of cards and was inscribed with DIPLOMATIC SHIELD SECURITY SYSTEM. Below this title was the symbol for Global Community and beneath it,: HOLOGRAMIC BOOK OF RINGS.

My curiosity reached its peak. I put the cigar down and carefully opened the little book. I saw that there were no actual pages, just nine touch-sensitive buttons and two black finger rings. Above the rings was a small screen or lens. Each button was marked with a Chinese character.

I put my finger to the top character. The pad became warm and instead of applying more pressure I let my finger sit for a few seconds. Each button became illuminated and the Book of Rings came alive. The circular lens swirled with electric color. The light became so intense that I scooted back a foot and stared in fascination. A small man, rather the image of a man, appeared from the book. Three feet tall, Asian, bald, and dressed in orange. The hologram addressed me directly and as if I were a Diplomat.

"Ambassador Gus Cast, on behalf of the International Free Community, I congratulate you for using these rings as identification and non-lethal defense. I am assigned to assist you in their use. I will instruct you in Xi Sui Jing so that you may become bonded with these devices by being purged of delusion and attachment from the mind, as well as internal pollutants from the body. These exercises are necessary so that you may use the technology of the Rings to harness electromagnetic forces. Place a ring on each thumb. After twenty four hours of wearing them you may find an open and private location to begin your training."

The instructor placed his fist into his open hand and bowed before zapping out.

∗　　　∗　　　∗　　　∗

Each night I was welcomed to a different campfire and often entertained with an animated story. The tale of tracking a jumping mouse could go on for several hours and was filled with more adventures and humor than any tale told in film or print. I shared stories as well, and discovered my own myth in the process. Fire-lit faces watched with slack jaws and listened intently about urban survival. Each morning I took my sun hat and walked off alone to train with the Book of Rings.

Every completed lesson was one step closer to the final San Jiao Da Li; The Triple Burner Flows Smoothly. I could visualize the internal energy, the Chi power, circulating in my body like the shape of a yin yang. It alternated between full and empty, and up and down.

Magnetic fields mysteriously shape our physical world. My body often tingled with fine currents of electricity. When I felt ready I asked the skin-walking children for help.

By putting my palms together, the thumb rings connected and started the opening of the energy gate. Within a few moments an invisible field radiated around my body. I invited young Malik and Catherine to throw pebbles at me. They crouched behind a boulder and giggled in the joy of this new game. First it seemed as if the small rocks were hitting me and bouncing off my skin. Soon, as the shield's strength grew, the stones deflected at an arm's length from my body. The incredible combination of martial and physical sciences kept me safe.

The kids of this desert world were remarkable in their ability to flow and blend with the landscape. These little ones could thrive where society's adults would suffer and die. They were truly of the earth, born off the grid and surrounded by the reality of spirit.

They were unlike any people I had ever met. I trusted them with my training and felt that all their special qualities and sensitivities to the world were giving me hope for the future. In some way these sacred little ones were going to change the world. For now they were outlaws, illegal aliens of the United Free community.

My final day in the wilderness came quickly. There were no teary-eyed good-byes. A silent understanding that we were all connected filled the air. The notion that we would be with each other again surrounded us when we hugged one another and kissed each other's cheeks.

Finder led the night-hike back to the barn. In the morning Basil and I would meet Cowboy-Kid, and quickly reintegrate into town life.

*   *   *   *

The post office's conditioned air turned my skin bumpy and made the clerk's perfume stay stagnant and smell strong. Another letter from Alexander assured us of our youngest brother's survival and made us both look forward to the day we could see him again. The Country Café's coffee tasted good, but I could detect additives and even a trace of soap left in the mug's pores. I could hear the traveling of electricity in the building's lighting. The purity of wilderness had sharpened my senses. The crowd was the usual. They seemed half-awake, moving through their day unaware of so much.

A new character walked into the middle of my observations. This guy stood out loudly, even to those with a butter-knife level of awareness. He was dark-skinned, light on his feet, and accompanied by a gun-sniffer. The robot had folded its body by his stool and had become a lump of silent steel on the floor. He ordered coffee and pie and slouched on the counter like a regular guy. He wasn't like the cops I was used to in the city. Regardless of his unusually mellow demeanor, it was clear that we were sharing space with a SAMURAI.

This SAM was probably one of the lone-wolves I had heard about over late-night drinks in the PANKRATION Club. The myth about wandering SAMURAIs was that they knew no greater pleasure than helping people they did not know. A wanderer was always too far away from backup to call for help. These were the types of warriors they made comic books about.

I sensed something else about this guy. He had an agenda but was trying his hardest to appear as if he was just passing through. When Sergeant Omni walked in it didn't matter what I or any of the other patrons thought of this drifter. Bring a gun-sniffer into Omni's hangout and there was going to be trouble.

A carpet of tension unrolled in the café when Omni removed his black hat. Everyone in the restaurant watched his hard smile become a mouth of gritted teeth. I, however, saw something more. The image I perceived sent an old and familiar shiver through my bones.

There, standing behind the cyber-genetic behemoth, was the Red Demon whom I had once battled in the world of spirits. I was sober and awake, yet as clear as the waters of Dripping Rock he stood before me; red and naked and half smiling at me. He was not here for me, though. The demon had chosen someone else.

The demon placed its hands on the Marine's shoulders and I watched Omni's awkward moment become one of pure rage. The creature whispered its dark message into his ear, and Omni's massive chest heaved in anger. His one-eyed glare perused the room and fell upon his New Navoon Legion with disappointment. Basil idly lit his pipe; I was the demon's only witness.

Lulu attempted to water down the tense scene with coffee. "Well, you gonna stand their looking handsome all night, or c'mon in so's I can git you some pickled pinto bean pie?"

Replacing the cover on his perfect spikes, Omni looked at his men with high beams of guilt. The evil spirit stepped out with an eerie, long-chinned grin in my direction. The sound of cups being put down and forks hitting plates filled the room. Six patrons got up as Omni pronounced his parting remark, aiming his words at the gun-sniffer. "I don't eat with devils!"

The door slammed and everyone, including Basil, seemed slightly relieved that violence was somehow avoided. Coffee got slurped, burgers got lifted, and the café resumed its business.

The SAM was now the one who was noticeably upset. I lifted an eyebrow to Basil, signaling him to monitor the peculiar situation. The cop jumped out of his stool and bent his head in the direction of the robotic canine.

"Damn you! Hi-tech garbage! Blow my cover!" He proceeded to kick the machine and shout, "Get out of here you worthless...*computer!*"

The dog, in strict obeisance to its master, stood on all fours and rocketed past the screen door. The SAM shook his head in apparent disgust and mumbled to himself from behind his coffee mug. I seemed to be the only one focusing on his quiet tirade. I noticed the flat microphone suctioned to his voice box. Without being heard, the unknown cop was transmitting his whispered words to another location.

My hands folded themselves under the table and the *Kuji-Kiri* focused me. As my fingers pointed down and became interlaced, the sounds of the room vanished and only the cop's covert dialogue remained. I heard him; somehow I knew he said, "Follow them and remain undetected. Full visual intel required."

Outside, as the men started up their trucks, the robot peered at them with digital optics. When the vehicles took off the dog obeyed its commands. It took chase, and ran undetected at forty or so miles an hour. It would latch on to one of the vehicle's bottoms when it could, it would stick like a tick does to human skin.

A few moments later I was keeping my observations under wraps and half-listening to Cowboy-Kid talk about the "pertiest little chick I picked up last week in Salt Lake." Basil and I walked out, and I noticed the heavy metal dog's tracks in the gravel. Then the horrible demonic image began to weigh heavy on my mind. I stopped and turned, telling Basil and the Kid, "Guys, I have to go back inside the café for a second."

As I did an about-face the cop stepped out of the restaurant. The guys froze as I approached the stranger.

"Excuse me."

"Yes?"

"I know what, or…who you are."

"You do."

"Yes, and this situation is…worse than it seems."

"It is."

"Yes, and, my name is Gus." With that I bowed and treated this officer in the manner I had been introduced to by some of my old training partners. "Please excuse my rudeness."

The SAM stood straight, slowly bowed, and came up with a big smile on his face. "My name is Officer Glazier, and I am a Wandering SAMURAI traveling through the Western States. I am familiar with you."

With this comment he retrieved a card-size screen from his pocket, than offered his hand to shake. When I joined the gesture of greetings he held my hand in his gloved grip and eyed the screen which was in his other.

"Hello, Constantine Cast. Friend of Peace."

The thumb rings worked.

✳ ✳ ✳ ✳

We talked in the parking lot. Beneath the stars, SAMURAI Glazier informed me of Homeland Defense's plans to investigate small militia groups throughout Utah. He wanted to assure me that there was nothing to worry about this evening. Before he could finish his explanation, a combat helicopter flying west thundered over our heads.

"You see Gus, one operation has already been activated. This will be handled by Homeland Commandos."

I rubbed my goatee as if it itched and tried to feel that all was safe. Inside, my vision would not allow me such assurance. My uncertainty came out in words. "It's not enough. I can't explain it, but it's just not right."

The SAMURAI stared deep into my eyes and nodded his head. "Okay, I don't have the intel on what they're holding, but antiquated firearms are no match for a combat team in battle armor. But…if it makes you feel better, I'll head over there myself."

He handed me a remote viewing screen. I stared into the little monitor's fuzzy picture.

"It'll clear up when my dog starts walking."

He trusted me with the gun-sniffer's information.

140   Naked Among the Tombs

Basil heard everything, and made a tactical recommendation to the International Policeman. "It'll be faster if you cut through the Warren."

"The Warren?" asked the cop.

Basil looked reluctant and sad as he said, "If it will save Omni's life, and avoid bloodshed, maybe you can take him down without a fight."

I replied, "Just follow us."

He agreed, "Right."

*   *   *   *

Before Omni's engine was cool the dog let go and fell into the dirt. It rolled smoothly into a shadow and transformed into an electric sleuth. I saw through its eyes on the small screen. It moved through penned cattle and photographed barns, sheds, and garages until it finally scrutinized the building occupied by humans. It detected its real target: guns.

In one room the men of the Legion were gathering and loading bullets. The guns were a far cry from what these combat veterans had used in foreign wars. The fact was that according to global law, they were destructive and illegal in civilian hands. The Home Defense base in Colorado viewed the situation with scrutiny and made the decision to put the King's Ranch on their list for this night's arrests.

I watched Omni load a Mini-14 rifle and heard him shout to his men through the gun sniffer's hardware, "I would that ye should know that I fought much with the sword to preserve my people!" He finished his Book of Mormon sermon just before the camera's transmission fizzled out.

*   *   *   *

We were making record time, followed by Glazier's motorcycle, to get to the Warren. At King's Ranch a single Homeland Security chopper, led by the dog's uploaded data, hovered menacingly over the New Navoon Legion's stronghold. Global Police had deemed Omni's zealots to be an illegal militia that had to be disbanded.

Now we viewed the mission through the helmet-cam lenses of the chopper's crew. The small viewer I was given glowed in my lap and vibrated with the sound of coming catastrophe.

The many garage doors of the ranch building flew open and a virtual army of beat-up three and four wheelers, motor bikes, and pick-up trucks rolled out to face the floating threat. With a wave of his hat the sergeant signaled his cavalry to accelerate. A voice resounded from the ship's speakers and was louder than the propellers.

"Stop your vehicles! We are under right and authority International! You have violated Global firearms laws and must surrender yourselves immediately!"

The voice finished and the chopper hovered. The vehicles soon stopped at the lip of a deep and impassable canyon. The ATVs and 4-wheelers formed a circle, like a wagon caravan of old in defense of themselves in a once-untamed land. The sergeant leaped from one of the quads. His patch was off and a green light marked the space where his eyeball once sat. The heavily-muscled commander wore fatigue pants, a green T-shirt and combat boots. He held his rifle, and a lasso hung from his belt. He yelled back to the *"whup, whup, whup"* sound of the turning helicopter.

"We will surrender to you!" the commander boomed as the flying machine listened with its audio equipment. The stoic cowboy troops were twenty strong. They all followed their leader by dismounting and dropping and sliding their weapons. Lever-action rifles, shotguns, and scoped hunting weapons looked toy-like in the shadow of the flying war chariot above. The New Navoon Legion formed a circle of surrender with hands held high while their engines were left running. The chopper began its descent and a dusty wind hid the sergeant's slow, careful, retreat.

"Your service to your country will be taken into account, Sergeant!"

The right to bear arms had long since been revoked. Even as ranchers, Omni's men needed internationally-registered permits. For the sergeant and his group, such a limitation on human rights was the fulfillment of prophecy.

On Omni's signal his unarmed citizen-soldiers removed the sturdy cable ropes that hung from their waists. Through the intense and dusty winds they twirled their lassos overhead. They let the loops fly suddenly, and one by one tied themselves to the chopper's landing skids. The sergeant knew that more oppressors would be coming, and this was the first wave of his counterattack. Perfectly-executed hoops continued to whistle through the air and cinch tightly onto their marks. In mere seconds, the Legion had the ropes tied to half of their vehicles and were remounted and driving off.

The five armored commandos on board looked befuddled and even humored by the Legion's tactics. I watched them from their helmet-cams' perspectives on my small screen. They were joking when one said, 'Looks like we're getting hog-tied boys!" just before cocking their laser-burst weapons. Before they could take aim the vehicles had driven away from the canyon and then quickly doubled back causing the chopper to fight going into a tailspin.

The youngest looking of the soldiers, who had enjoyed the rush of being near the open door without being strapped-in watched the scene below with confusion. "What the fuck!" were the last words Lieutenant Reeves uttered before hitting the ground and losing consciousness.

"Stabilize this bird!" shouted the crew chief.

It was too late. The Legion had successfully turned the chopper, and the vehicles were now pulling it straight toward the dark and deadly abyss. One by one, the skilled veterans leaped from their trucks and quads. The vehicles were acting like a bola would to enwrap the legs of a deer and bring it down hard. The cowboys rolled to safety like Hollywood stuntmen and stood to watch the weight and momentum of their ghost riders pull the helicopter and remaining crew down to their doom.

*   *   *   *

The Kid's truck came to a dusty and screeching halt, and SAMURAI Glazier's bike lifted rock and dirt to make a dusty stop. We all climbed atop the cab of the truck to stare off into the distant canyon. The explosion we witnessed summarized the tragedy that had just occurred.

Glazier spoke directly into his wristwatch. Perhaps prodded by my dark prediction, he called for massive retaliation and utmost caution against an armed and aggressive enemy. He told me that reinforcements could take up to an hour. The SAMURAI was extremely concerned with possible captives and potential victims that the Legion might find in its warpath. Glazier had calculated the high likelihood of Omni targeting the closest armory, and knew that the quickest route would put the Warren in the way.

*   *   *   *

The explosions were multiple and massive, loud enough to wake the downed commando from his painful blackout. His was the last camera running and the movie he shot was one of horror. The armor he wore had apparently preserved his bones and protected him from mortal injury. I think he felt that if he could get his wind back, he would be ready to fight. Groping for his weapon, he found only its smashed remains. His combat gear included back-up arms, however. Rising to one knee, he armed wrist-rockets and scanned the perimeter for attackers.

Before he could rise to full stance the wind was knocked from his body again. This time his concussion was at the hands of the battle-crazed sergeant.

"Hughhh!" gasped Reeves, helpless as Omni tore at his armor with his bare hands, disarming him quickly and punishing his exposed flesh with hammering fists. Explosive flames rose from the deep ravine, and the men who surrounded the beaten commando, bathed in horrifying firelight, looked as if they had just leaped from hell, and were ready to spread fire all over the world. They hooted and hollered as the panting Omni planted his boot into the captive's jaw. It sounded as if his mandible had been cracked before he was rendered unconscious.

"Don't celebrate yet boys!"

The men instantly quieted and stood to attention.

"Riggs!"

"Yes sir!"

"Secure the prisoner on your vehicle. Anar!"

"Sir!"

"Send the rewired canine ahead of us and monitor video surveillance!"

"Yes sir!"

"Gentlemen," he said to all his troops. "There is no time to waste. The devils will be comin' down on us. We must hit Fieldridge arsenal now and arm ourselves for Phase Two. We have expected this for a long time. Their roundups have begun, but we will beat them back with fire and brimstone and the sword of righteousness!"

Omni's glowing green eye came close to the camera and filled my screen. Then the helmet-camera flew through the air as the New Navoon Legion leader hurled it across the desert.

"Wooo! Yeah! Hoooahhh!"

The war cries were impassioned, and there was no doubt of their conviction to fight and die if necessary against the new order of the world that they were being left out of. These battle-scarred heroes had become pariahs of the System. They who were outcasts had now become outlaws.

*　　　*　　　*　　　*

The barn was dimly lit. Unsure of the explosion's cause, the Warrenites were on high alert and ready to run, hide, and survive whatever catastrophe might befall them. Basil's close friends rose from the shadows and crawled from the tunnel as their unofficial team leader sucked his lower lip against his teeth to mimic the squeak of a mouse. This was the Warren's signal for safety.

Rita was the first to speak, "Basil, what's going on?"

Officer Glazier responded and hoped that his urgency would be contagious. "Explain later, all of you people have to evacuate and not look back."

Basil comforted Rita by reaching for her hand and gently pulling her into his grasp.

"Who is this guy?" questioned Annie, as she rose from one of the bunks. The SAM lashed out, purposely sounding emotional and intense. "It doesn't matter who I am right now!" Looking at his wristwatch he continued, "A surveillance robot is headed this way according to my Handler System. The same people who just made things go boom are using it. If you value your safety and the well being of your friends, you will curtail your understandable curiosities and get out of the way of what is coming through here."

Silence darkened the room as storm clouds rolled in to dim the desert starlight. Someone shouted out a panicked response. "But Omni is a friend to the Warren! They wouldn't harm us, this is our home."

Someone else got their opinion out with a shaky voice, "His Legion will bring the heat here, we'll be caught in the middle, and the Skin—"

Basil interrupted, and spoke with decisiveness. "Grab your Possible-sacks. Don't forget ponchos. Finder…take us south. Single-file and in silence. We leave in two."

No one protested my brother's guiding words. They all knew his integrity and the high value he placed on personal freedom. If Basil wanted the community to run, then there was good reason behind it.

Fritz, who usually stayed quiet and observant, interrupted the group's panicked preparations with his own thoughtful question. "The dog, if it's a gun-sniffer set for surveillance, will find us, and the Legion will be following it. Then the fight will still fall on us. Even if we don't get hurt tonight, how many of us registry-dodgers will survive investigation?"

Basil maintained his cool, but knew that his friend spoke the truth. "Nothing we can do now Fritz. The man says we gotta run."

Glazier exhaled and looked at the dog's high speed rate of travel on the tiny screen before responding. "Your friend is quite right. It is their scout and some force will be tracking it. But before anyone can disable it, the dog will alarm its new keepers, and we must assume that they will react with hostility."

"So we are fucked!" interjected Finder.

The Viking raised his lance and said, "Unless someone takes the mutt out."

Finder fired back by finishing his blood brother's sentence. "A _person_ will set this thing's alarm off man!"

A hooded figure spoke from a blind spot in the room. Everyone was surprised when they heard, "A person, yes; not me." The shadow figure dove into the tapestry and was tearing through the tunnel before Basil could realize what was happening.

"Focus up!" Putting a hand on Fritz's shoulder, Basil continued to re-center the group by saying, "We stick to the plan and work with what we got. No more questions. Finder, let's head out."

*　　　*　　　*　　　*

Omni was probably looking up at the blackening sky as his men tied the incapacitated commando to his truck's hood. Listening to my remote I heard the zealot leader bark, "Tie 'em up good. We don't want this buck slidin' off. We keep all our remaining vehicles in tight formation this night so's this little sellout soldier boy will keep those black birds from firing on us."

The sergeant's command was twisted but accurate. The Security Forces would not fire initially for fear of hitting their own investment. Lieutenant Reeves was badly hurt and his armor encased him like a shell on a dying beetle. Its nanocircuitry was still operational despite the exoskeleton's battered appearance. Reeve's vital signs were the only ones from his squad's still registering at the Colorado base.

Homeland Security was hurriedly dealing with the whole situation by shuffling around resources. They relayed Reeve's vitals to the scene's closest contact. As the Warrenites disappeared into the night, SAMURAI Glazier received the confirmation of the solo survivor. He reacted in the only way his training would permit him to.

*　　　*　　　*　　　*

Basil brought up the rear of the escape line and had counted heads before beginning the steady, controlled jog. I stopped in front of him and Basil let the troop go in order to find out why I had paused.

"Gus, what are you doing?"

"I'm going back."

"That SAMURAI can handle himself."

"Whatever happens, Basil, don't be sad."

He looked at me as if I had just finished something. Then he gripped my forearm and let me grip his. "When you're ready…" he said.

I squeezed and our arms became one unbreakable rope. "I know. I'm always welcome."

We both looked up unto the pregnant night sky. Our hands slid back and we ran in opposite directions.

*   *   *   *

Glazier was mounting his bike when I caught up with him. The SAMURAI did not question my choice. He only assessed his own battle plan in light of a new variable.

The gun-sniffer, now wired to work for Omni, moved at half speed and turned its head from side to side like a hunting cat. The screen I still held showed everything the dog could see, including a controller card that was protruding from its neck. Duct tape supported the Legion's guerrilla technician's handiwork.

The robotic dog took in the world through its camera optics and sonar barks. It ignored nature, as it was programmed to do, and did not alarm when a coyote matched its pace. The wild dog ran side by side with the mechanized one. In mid-crouch, while moving, Oso's black blade slashed and stabbed at any exposed circuitry. Within minutes the robot was down. The last sign of electric life faded from its digital eyes.

Glazier's monitor told him his machine's transmission had ended. I watched him then peer into the desert. I guessed he was thinking of the shadow man who took the mission. Then SAMURAI Glazier appeared to feel a surge of hope.

I asked him, "What's the plan?"

"The plan? They have a captive. I will ride out to them and surrender."

"Surrender? Officer Glazier, no offense but...."

"Gus, there are six good men lying dead out there because I underestimated a threat. One soldier has survived and I will do whatever must be done to save him. I will offer myself as a trade. They are unlikely to accept. Then, I will attempt to dispatch their leader. If you feel it necessary to help and are willing to...go to war, then your services will be greatly appreciated."

He dismounted from his bike and bowed. He stood and awaited my acknowledgment.

"I'm in. What do I do?"

The SAM smiled and lifted the seat on his cycle, revealing a cache of tools and weapons. My eyes grew wide in amazement at Glazier's war gear. "But, I thought you guys don't use weapons," I said.

"Gus, like I told you before, we Wanderers are different. We need to be prepared for anything, including battle. Now, we don't have much time. Do you have experience with firearms?"

My surprise magnified when I was handed a sniper's pistol. "Yes. Well, not much. More from video games."

"That's all right. This weapon does most of the work. It's more computer than anything else. You have to find your target in the scope, press this record-control, then it doesn't matter if you point it behind you because the smart bullet will still find the bad-guy you need to put down."

I tried to separate myself from the reality of Glazier's comments. I was going to commit myself to helping this warrior by being a warrior. My intent was to maybe help that captive and keep the fight away from the Warren and the heat off the Warrenites. Just maybe this was the special purpose that I was looking for all along.

Trickles of rain had begun to fall. As directed, I wore my hat and poncho in case I had to be sitting for a while. We rode quickly toward the West. When I recognized the primary cover that I needed, I tapped the motorcycle driver on the shoulder so I could stop and prepare. Glazier was happy with my choice of hiding spots and was impressed that I could disappear so completely beneath a common looking sage brush.

The plan was simple and explained coldly. Glazier would ride up and meet the Legion's caravan with a white flag. The cop would surrender, and if he had the opportunity, take out the individual who controlled the militia. If the SAM could not take out Omni, then it would be my turn to fire a single, hopefully untraceable bullet into the outlaw leader's unsuspecting head. I would do this before retreating down the Warren's tunnel to safety.

The best possible scenario was that the Legion would be thrown into a state of panic and their direct route to restock their arsenal would be delayed. This would give enough time for Homeland Defense choppers to arrive and do the job that the commando team had failed to do.

*   *   *   *

Omni's soldier was probably still tinkering with the downed dog's snowy video monitor they had rigged up when the robot was rewired. With my gun's powerful scope I could see the irate commander grab the monitor from its user's hands and hurl it into the dampening sands. Before he could tell his passenger that they didn't need the dog and that he should keep his human eyes peeled, something caught his attention. The sergeant slammed on his breaks and reached for his gun as the waving white cloth of a parked motorcyclist appeared in his headlights.

Glazier showed both hands to the Legion in a sign of passivity. The renegade vehicles rolled into formation and all their weapons secured their perimeter. I watched the scene through the telescopic night-ready lens. I saw Glazier drop to his knees and crawl, with his hands still raised, toward the pointing rifles.

Omni's mouth moved in an obvious commanding fashion. Glazier dropped to his belly and three men ran toward the surrendering cop. Glazier's legs were folded so that his heels touched his backside. One man sat on his curled up feet while the butt ends of two rifles hammered into his shins. Mechanically the men made the same devastating blows to each of their prisoner's arms. I struggled with myself to move my gaze from my new partner's pain and onto the sergeant's skull.

The outlaws shuffled in front of my potential shot and Glazier was methodically strapped onto a truck's hood just as the beaten commando had been. Omni's green eye scanned the land and sky. He was paranoid, and suspicious of the quick capture of an elite International Police Officer. Finally it happened; he came into my view, and I tried to paint him. I eased the pistol's trembling with breath control and stared hard into my target. Glazier had set it up this way all along, I supposed. It had to be right. The storm clouds were swooping lower and the drizzle turned into drops.

I tried to find a deeper purpose in this act. I tried to think that in taking out this group's leader I would be doing something good. The bullet would do the killing, would terminate this monster who tore helicopters from the sky. I wouldn't be killing this man who bore the scars of war and led men who limped and gripped guns with clawed pincers. I wouldn't kill this man who was no enemy of mine, the bullet would do the killing. I held the pistol and my thumbs touched and my finger reached above the trigger to lock the bad-guy in as my smart bullet's target.

All I had left to do was to squeeze the instrument. All my struggles must have been to lead me to this moment. But, what about what the young Sensei had told me not to forget? What about his realization on the battlefield of blood that he had waited in life and in death to finally share? What about his warning to me and the lesson that was so important I had to become a new person in order to receive it? What about his profound experience of human suffering that reached out to me from the grave and told me to never take another human life?

For once it is done, you are never the same, and the rest of your days will be spent climbing out from the hole of despair which the killing has dug.

In that instant the gun I held went dead. I stared through a dark tunnel and wondered what kind of advanced SAMURAI weapon would just run out of juice at such a crucial time. The rain pitter-pattered on my hat and my mind analyzed the noise. The rain echoed as I held the pistol from within the branches of the sage brush and pointed toward the circle of car lights.

Something about the rain, and the hopelessness of the situation made me want to rise from the hole in the ground and stand in the downpour. I climbed out, and still clutching the weapon, and saw the water bounce off an invisible shield around my body.

The rings! The rings had touched while I gripped the gun and the electromagnetic current shorted the weapon's circuitry while creating a shield of protection around my body.

Engines revved. The Legion had seen me surface. I threw the useless weapon behind me and reconnected my hands in the prayer position. The war caravan was blinding me with headlights. I had no time to concoct any semblance of a backup plan. I was starting to wish I had stayed in my hole. I simply stood in the rain. I envisioned the teachings of the little glowing Sifu.

The trucks and quads stayed tight with Omni's jeep in front center. On either side of the leader were the vehicles that sported the gory trophies. I fought to control my heart rate amid such horror. The SAMURAI pulled his head up and looked on me without judgment. I moved my eyes from the captured warrior and stared directly at the sergeant.

Unbelievably, the scene became more horrific when the Red Demon, accompanied by the silken-robed Lord Hachiman, rose from the jeep's backseat. The demons were grinning and my focus shifted like a pinball ricocheting through my body. The sergeant aimed his weapon at me. I am sure I appeared to him as something sinister. After all, I was the mysterious one. He saw someone shrouded by a conical green hat and draping raingear. An unseen force was deflecting water drops from around me as I held my hands together like a wizard in ceremony. The element of surprise should have belonged to me.

Because he didn't understand what he saw, Omni's first reaction was a violent one. In anticipation of a potential SAMURAI trick he aimed and shot.

Bang! One shot rang out accompanied by the words, "Die, Warlock!"

Glazier's head lay back on the hood. I knew that his heart's breaking overwhelmed the pain in his shattered limbs. He blamed himself for being the cause of another casualty.

I stumbled and rolled backward over the bush. I disappeared behind the plant and wondered if I was dying. As my hands separated and hit the dirt, rain struck my face for the first time that night. I thought then that if I wasn't mortally wounded, that maybe I could just be still in the downpour. Maybe the whole militia would pass me by. Omni's yelled order of "Make sure he's dead!" canceled out my hopes. Despair overtook me.

Before I could totally give up and roll over in a puddle, I sensed something moving near me. A hand grasped my wrist. The man in the coyote's fur stood over me and gripped onto my arm. Oso pulled my hands together and got me to stand. The snout touched my hat and the voice beneath it said, "If you have ever believed, now is the time to know."

I felt the energy move through my center and radiate forth. I was strong and knew that fear, not force, had knocked me down. I stepped over the plant and advanced toward my attacker without thought. The Legion's lights and rifles were all aimed at me. Omni sprang from his seat and stood on the hood of his jeep shouting, "He's mine! He's mine! The witch is mine!"

The outlaws held their fire as their leader took aim through the rain. The SAMURAI breathed deep and I sensed he had decided to not calculate the odds. I felt that instead he chose to pray to a force that lay above the black pouring clouds. Thunder bellowed and lightning illuminated the area. I saw the demons' expressions change to pure rage. As the red devil whispered to Omni, I watched Hachiman drag a bound Pasito from behind the jeep. He knocked my Sensei to his knees.

Bang!

A single round exploded from Omni's Mini-14. It ricocheted off of an invisible force field just more than an arm's length in front of me. Pasito looked up, and I witnessed the same concerned eyes that I had met in my vision. Hachiman drew a sword and pushed Pasito prostrate with his foot.

"Die, Demon!" yelled Sergeant Omni with a voice that resonated with both anger and fear.

Bang! Bang! Bang! Bang!

The weapon fired on automatic and as the magazine emptied, my energy field grew. Spent bullets were scattered directly in front of the jeep and rain bounced off in an enormous aura that encircled me. Unexpectedly Omni's legs locked. He screamed as his body took on enormous weight and fell straight back like a toppled statue. The headlights, in an instant, were extinguished. The green light of Omni's mechanical eye fizzled out. All engines went silent and suddenly the entire war party stood without being touched by the rain. The giant, invisible force shielded us all.

Everything was consumed by the darkness of the stormy night save for the flash of frequent lightning bolts. All electronics ceased and I stood as a serene circuit for the earth's power. As Oso stepped from behind me, revealing his human form, the Legion was hit with another effect of the electro-magnetic field. My efforts had summoned a Plasma. Every human in the path of this ionized gas experienced a rush of serotonin release. Even Omni, whose mechanized body parts were heavy and lifeless, began to smile in the beauty of a pleasant hallucination.

His soldiers lay down their weapons. I must have appeared to them as angelic when I stepped closer. Rain drops pelted the dome of energy and made a water show which was back-dropped by fantastic rainbow lights, like an aurora borealis. A fantastic spectral phenomenon caused by a magnetic ground surge danced around the dome and before the awestruck eyes.

I watched the surrender unfold in the steady illuminations of ozone-smelling electricity. *Crack!* went the thunder and the spirit of the Sensei broke from his bonds. The naked red beast leaped from the jeep like a predacious bug, but Pasito was too quick. He grabbed Hachiman's katana, spun, and split his attacker in half at the waist.

Seeing his venomous son writhe in pain, the Lord Hachiman backed up in disgust. The ground opened up with a wave of the dark master's hand and swallowed him and his grotesque, squirming child. They were returned to a place of ultimate darkness.

Many of the outlaw marines knelt and put their palms together. Tears flowed. Prayers of redemption were muttered. I watched the Sensei flash a smile before performing a quick bow and disappearing. The shape-shifter who had picked me up and given me hope had vanished as well, swallowed by the great mystery of night.

✳　　✳　　✳　　✳

I was sitting with SAMURAI Glazier and Lieutenant Reeves when the armed commandos cautiously approached.

As helicopters pressed in on garden plots, their search beams lit up the strange scene of surrendering renegade warriors. I ignored the heavy rain and wind and did not listen to the arresting voice that boomed from a megaphone. My mind heard only my own silent prayer of thanks which traveled upward through the dark and down pouring storm.

CHAPTER 13

▼

JOY TO THE WORD

Demetrios's door was open, and a walking cane hung from its knob. The lamps were off but everything was dimly visible in the sunlight which leaked through the curtains. He lay still on his back. The sheet draped over a bony figure. His rhythmic breathing sounded mechanical.

I searched for clues of Demetri's status. My eyes fell upon a machine next to his bed. A flexible tube was attached to a mask over his mouth and nose. An accordion like pump rose and fell with sucking and wheezing sounds.

One thought, one word, one nightmare played out. Apocalypse repeated over and over. All my lessons were just dust on the chalkboard, blown away, and covered over by rage. My anger rose and fell in the pulse of my clenched fists, and squeezed itself into an oozing sadness.

The air was thick with a lethargy that was broken up only by the faint bite of incense. A plate of little perfumed cones intermixed with a bundle of sage and cedar had never been burned but still gave off the mild smell of good medicine. The war god had already visited my brother, and no amount of sweet smells could undo what had been done.

No illusions here.

The gun, the bomb, the heavy tear.

The postcard I'd sent home was tacked to the wall.

A bottle of purple liquor stood beneath the bed.

- 153 -

Outside, the snow was cascading down, accumulating, and covering tracks. I sat in the chair and tried to enter a state of sustained thoughtlessness until my brother got up.

The pump was distracting, Demetri's situation too disturbing, my memory cloudy. Things did not make sense. I couldn't meditate and even felt a bit queasy. I stared at him for a while. I remembered him as a kid. It seemed like the last time I saw him we were getting ready to face the end of the world together. In Basil's tracks, and with cub-scout canteens, we were going to embrace a radically different millennium.

When it was all over everyone but Basil had bought into the big lie of a United Free Planet. We all wanted to believe that an intelligent society could save us from disaster. Personal responsibilities fell away and were picked up by the courts. Materialism reigned and the world's spirits sank into vats of collagen and credit and collateral damage. We had turned our backs on the important things that survival living might have taught us.

The new millennium had been our chance to change direction. We blew it. Then we blew it up. When we wanted, we took; when we doubted, we killed. My blinders were off, now. This guy in front of me did not need to suffer this. No one does. I can't justify it anymore.

We have these short lives, these brief moments to share and celebrate, and I just don't think that preserving and perpetuating a high level of gluttony and turn-ons is worth killing for. I am sure if the dead could break their code of silence, even for a brief moment, than this would be their message.

On the other side of apocalypse is salvation. Most of us are looking away from both, and settling for limbo. I wasn't settling anymore. I'd rather be a hungry vagabond then a numbed citizen of this new Rome.

My reminders are in my poems. I close my eyes when I begin to write, and travel to a pure place.

I read from my journal for a while. It calmed me. The sucking sound had its own rhythm and I tracked it. For a moment I managed to stop thinking.

*   *   *   *

"What are ya reading Gus?" He was sitting up, and not as skinny as I thought. Actually, he looked good, almost radiant, in fact.

"It's just my journal. Poems and stuff." I felt small and warm beneath his light. He was aglow with confidence. "Demitch, you're okay?"

"Right now I am. And right now, so are you."

"Want to hear a poem?"

I never broke bread like this before, not with friends, or teachers, or anyone. Not with this stuff that came out warm from the ovens of my real self. But it seemed the right time. I was nervous. My audience was waiting patiently, glowing, like a plant about to receive water. I poured it out slowly, like a Skin Walker stalking through the desert in search of a new guise. I imagined the rhythm of a shape-shifter transforming itself in the ancient dance.

*   *   *   *

When finished I started to close my journal only to realize I had never opened it.

Silence. I couldn't even hear the breathing machine anymore. Demetri was smiling just before the vision ended.

My eyes opened and I was startled to feel Muso jump into my lap. The cat yawned and snuggled into my hands. As I pressed my face against his orange coat I was startled again.

"Gus…" Demetri whispered through the muffling face-mask. "That cat never said 'hi' to me like that," he joked, with apparently great effort.

The respirator pumped.

"We've been through a lot together," stumbled out of my mouth.

Muso hopped off and lightly hit the floor as I stood and watched Demetrios slowly remove his cloudy mask. He took nearly a minute to turn and put his feet down. I could tell he wasn't comfortable in his movements. As I approached, Demetri extended his pale, sticklike arms. His bulbous elbows looked fractured.

I feared that my affection might hurt him, but despite his emaciated body, his hug was solid. As I lifted my head from my brother's shoulder I saw that his sunken cheekbones appeared to have raised and his mouth had sharpened into a smile.

Demetri sat back down and asked me to close the door before offering me a drink. We tapped crusty glasses. His ashen complexion achieved a brief coloring after the shot. I hoped that his deathly-gray pallor would never return.

"Thanks for the postcard, bro."

"Thanks for reading it."

"You kidding me…wish I was there with you man…there's no finer thing a person can do than to be free and searching for what really matters."

I tried not to sound condescending when I said, "I don't know if everybody else shares your high regard for wandering aimlessly."

156   Naked Among the Tombs

"Fuck everybody else, Gus!"

His excitement got him coughing and I handed him the tube and mask he was reaching for. He sucked in air and the thing made a fast spinning sound. After what seemed to be several minutes of breathing with the machine, the whirling of the respirator finally ended.

I was suddenly hyper-aware. Demetri recovered himself and looked at my shaken-up appearance thoughtfully. I was thinking of my own past afflictions when I said, "Maybe when you're ready, I'll take you to meet some friends of mine in the city."

"Oh yeah? That sounds real nice, Gus. I'd like that. But let's get back to the other thing now."

"What? The fact that I haven't worked in almost four years, and haven't been able to stop philosophizing long enough to have any semblance of direction in my life."

"Hand me that cane."

Giving him the polished stick, I offered a hand.

"I got it," he said before exhaling hard. Placing a hand on my shoulder he looked into my eyes and told me, "If the world had more philosophers and poets, maybe we would ask the 'why' before blowing up the 'what.'"

Looking down at his own feet he appeared to have to concentrate to take a first step. "C'mon now, let's go downstairs and get some grub. We got some catching-up to do."

Staring at the back of my brother's head slowed things down to a dizzy turtle crawl. We stopped at the bottom of the staircase.

"Gus...."

"What's up?"

"Thanks for reading me that poem."

While making our hobbled march, my memories swirled together as if in an artist's kit. Like a great spinning tornado of paint, the past spread itself onto the canvas of my mind. These were all my experiences, and they had led me to this moment.

✳   ✳   ✳   ✳

"You awake man?"

My pack? Still here. Awake? The bus station, must've dozed. It was all just a dream. "Yeah, I'm awake."

"Yer ride is leavin', man, meditate on the bus."

Street kid. Part of a tribe. The new species being born off the registry. His name was Frito. "What 'cha waitin' for Gus, time for you to go home. It'll be Christmas soon."

I had been teaching them martial arts. Internal for health because they had no medical coverage, and external for defense because their bodies were their only security.

"Final goodbyes, git on the bus, Gus," said Colleen. Her sixteen-year-old tattooed hands gesticulated something between a knockout punch and a goodbye hug.

"Cops, yo, let's break out," said a voice from behind the corner of the orange tile wall.

"It's cool," came out of Frito's clenched teeth. "They're SAMs. Gus is right with them."

He was correct. They wouldn't force us to leave. My ride was here, though. We got up together, and walked as one bundle of rags and backpacks. I put my hands together in the prayer position when I bowed to the SAMURAI.

"The 118, Newark-bound! Now boarding!"

Icy rain was pelting the pavement outside. The police would have kicked them out if I wasn't here. If they fought back, they'd be put through the System and eventually end up in a recruiter's office.

"It's comin down like a bastard out dere, man, wish I was rollin' out wit' you," said Aki, and bumped my shoulder with the controlled affection of a runaway.

"You want my ticket, Ak?"

"Naw man, come on now, quit teasing, you gots to go!"

"I'm not teasing." The ticket felt suddenly foreign, and I needed to get rid of it.

"It's cold out there, Gus," said Frito gently, "and yer family's waiting."

I froze for a moment, and scanned the crowd of holy faces. The glossy little paper in my hand became comical and it took everything in my power not to burst into laughter.

"He's cracking up, yo," someone observed with surprised interest.

"Aki, your bus is leaving," I fired out in an attempt to control the peculiar emotions which giggled up from some mad, free wellspring. My statement only made things funnier.

Aki reacted in a raised voice, "I ain't going to New Jersey, yo!"

She paused, and the group tightened into aware and serious postures.

"You all are my family, and the earth is my home," finished her thought.

"Support," said Frito, with deep sincerity that held an almost religious undertone.

The group nodded and whispered in countenance.

"You're right," I added, "even in the cold, icy rain, the earth is our home."

Everyone was smiling and waking up and releasing that mad, free feeling that could not be purchased anywhere but in the sweet cupboard of total surrender.

"That's it, Gus, even in the beautiful, icy-cold, skin-splitting rain, I'm at home," said the now upbeat Frito.

"Support!" someone said a little louder, punctuating the general feeling of transcendence and empowerment.

"Anyone want to go to New Jersey!" I blurted out as I raised the silly thing up high. The kids were cracking up and one of the old-time wanderers looked over and raised a fist in approval of our gathering. His toothless grin and Rip Van Winkle beard just put me over the top, and my laughter at having figured out the big joke of life resounded.

The SAMURAI turned, and moved toward our energetic huddle like sharks tracking blood. Even if I could talk my way out of it, I wasn't going to. The outside was waiting, and I knew just the tree to visit.

The doors kicked open and the wind and water invigorated me. The ticket was stuck in a wall tile now for anyone who needed it.

"You coming, Rip?" I shouted to the elder as the SAMs approached.

We sprinted and turned a few corners and huddled inside the great spruce that could actually hide and protect us until the sun came up.

A small candle-lantern marked the center of our squatter's circle and illuminated the cozy bird's nest above us. We whispered as we repositioned for warmth and comfort. Sandy, who was my equivalent in age and my senior in street experience, gripped my hand lightly and paused before she said, "I'm glad you're staying man."

Silence, but for the gentle cooing of the alert bird.

"Give us a beat Aki," I said, then pointing up at the nest, "and keep it soft."

She pushed out a beat as smooth and rhythmic as a snake swimming through warm mud. Our coniferous shelter was a fragrant natural cathedral. I closed my eyes, and let it out like I had in the dream.

Poems are my accomplishments,
not dark monuments that expose the lack of faith in spirit and the true fear of
death that torments us to mummify our bodies and lock up our lives in illusions
of safety and mandatory wives and husbands that rent hookers in dark seedy dives

to remember the youth that they never really had and to not die of a heart-attack when that kid says "Hey dad—who are you? Who am I? What happens when we die? Because I vaguely remember being with God before I met you" are the words of a kid that I actually knew, well, she was a friend's little niece, yeah this is the piece that I tend to forget when mistakes become weights and here comes the regret about not being where I am supposed to be and it seems self-defeating to think of the Buddhist-me whose every action has a reason even falling in love and trembling at the thought of having and holding then breaking her heart to escape being molded and missing the chance to do something great for nothing more real than potential's sweet sake the great evolution the icing and the cake then there's damnation the fiery lake the one Eve was led to by the blarney-tongued snake and greater than that is the idea of Good by definition its better therefore logic says we should choose the ideal, the best way to be which comes with temp- tation that's always hard to see at first for it has no mass we give it its power before it knocks us on our ass in the guise of an option a calculated risk "You mean if I take this blue pill I'll never get sick?" is a shortcut but this is the skinny, the Way is hard and side-tracks are many and your confusion may be illusion when you widen your gaze the off-trail is better so you spend a few days and have the experience for which nobody pays out-of-body, true Karate, the tingling in your back that rises up the spine when minute earthly particles become instru- ments of heavenly design and then you'll have the vision and be able to go out- side of the cave, Plato's allegory—the one filled with slaves, and they'll hate you for leaving their dark world of pain and your eyes hurt from sunlight but you've got everything to gain it's not as convenient when the shackles are gone you'll have to find your own way to the john and you will be alone for a time way out there in a universe so vast that a bear rests in the air and shines down at night when you're not scared of the planet that rises to greet your feet to let you know you are about to achieve immortality just before your brain, that hunk of meat, starts spinning and thinking churning dough into bread then it happens all of a sudden you think "What if I'm dead?" or never been born I'm still in the womb and when I do come out I'll be dropped off naked among tombs, gnashing my teeth, running back and forth looking for the thief who took away happiness and left me with no clothes on my back and froth on my lip I'm starving but nau- seous when voices ring out then all just goes silent and I want to shout but my voice is so meager these stones are so cold I read the inscription it says Never Lived Just Grew Old but old Ebenezer he had another chance to learn the new physics and fall in love with romance I got that chance and you know something so do you so throw out the punctuation and unlock the zoo let wild life run free

and talk to a tree first bow respectfully and ask your question be sincere and soon
you'll have the knowing that all you need is right here before you and behind you
beneath and above beauty walks with you its other name is Love without condi-
tions all embracing its in your eyes when you smile the poem I really meant to
write is about that little child whose mind is clear and still and quite silent it hears
the tree when it says:

Although I stand above tombstones
I am never alone
the light is so lovely
and makes us all grow
shining upon our heads
reflecting off the snow
feeding my branches
opening our seeds
man is a strange one
creating so many needs
when life is a miracle
just look at my leaves
falling gently through the air
without sadness or despair
this life is a cycle
and a tree's only care
is to reach for the warmth
the light that darkness cannot bear.

Somewhere within this maelstrom of awareness, between the violence of the
world and often next to ghosts and demons, swims the truth of words.

The words have saved me over and over again. They guided me and continue
to be a signpost toward my real self.

Words can make history palatable and bless us with prescience.

I know now that the word is buoyant. It can not wither away, and never gives
up. In scribbles and scratching, in songs and played out in all sorts of scenes, it
keeps on telling.

It will keep you afloat. Over the vast, fast-breaking waves of infinite tides,
there are stories being told, and poems are coming, and they will make you ready,
and you will be welcome.

THE END

978-0-595-36146-5
0-595-36146-3

Printed in the United States
40169LVS00005B/301-402